BEST MISTAKE EVER

CHRISTY MCKELLEN

B

Boldwood

First published in Great Britain in 2025 by Boldwood Books Ltd.

Copyright © Christy McKellen, 2025

Cover Design by Leah Jacobs-Gordon

Cover Images: Leah Jacobs-Gordon and Shutterstock

The moral right of Christy McKellen to be identified as the author of this work has been asserted in accordance with the Copyright, Designs and Patents Act 1988.

Every effort has been made to obtain the necessary permissions with reference to copyright material, both illustrative and quoted. We apologise for any omissions in this respect and will be pleased to make the appropriate acknowledgements in any future edition.

A CIP catalogue record for this book is available from the British Library.

Paperback ISBN 978-1-83617-007-5

Large Print ISBN 978-1-83617-006-8

Hardback ISBN 978-1-83617-005-1

Ebook ISBN 978-1-83617-008-2

Kindle ISBN 978-1-83617-009-9

Audio CD ISBN 978-1-83617-000-6

MP3 CD ISBN 978-1-83617-001-3

Digital audio download ISBN 978-1-83617-004-4

This book is printed on certified sustainable paper. Boldwood Books is dedicated to putting sustainability at the heart of our business. For more information please visit https://www.boldwoodbooks.com/about-us/sustainability/

Boldwood Books Ltd, 23 Bowerdean Street, London, SW6 3TN

www.boldwoodbooks.com

This one's for you, Soph. Keep being your brilliant self.

1

BEATRICE

My father has always made the job of being CEO of his own company look so simple, but then he's the tenacious type.

He's a brilliant man. *Brilliant*. But it's a lot to live up to.

When my sister, Delilah, and I were ten years old, he and my mother went through a really nasty divorce and it caused such a cataclysmic rift in our family, Dee and I are still living through the shockwaves of it. It tore our childhood apart, with each of us preferring a different parent to live with when my mother moved out of the family home and into an arty commune across town: me with Dad, Dee with Mum.

You see, despite being identical twins, Dee and I are polar opposites in personality. Our mother maintains that when the egg split, I got all of our father's 'shrewd genes' and Dee got her 'fun genes', which, despite our best efforts, seem to have informed the way we've lived our lives up till now.

Dee, for her part, seems to think I'm naturally good at everything I do, which is patently nonsense. I just work really hard and I don't give up easily.

Being good at things takes practice and discipline, but Dee

doesn't seem to be naturally predisposed to either of these things.

It's good to have her living nearby again though. Despite our differences, I've missed her while I've been away at university in London and she at art college in Exeter, and we've grown a lot closer since we've been living in the same city again.

It was great when, last year, she moved into a very tiny, but super cute, attic flat that I found for her a few streets away from me. She'd hoped Bath, where I settled after graduating, would be a better place to forge ahead with her dream of being an artist, after struggling to make it happen in Devon.

But it's not worked out so far.

Trouble is, she's not been able to stick at any of the jobs she's done to pay the bills since graduating either.

To be fair to her though, she's been trying hard to readjust her life's trajectory since our father laid into her about it at an excruciating family meal a few months ago.

Over the years, she's learnt to let his criticism of her go right over her head, but unfortunately, this time he caught her on a bad day.

She totally lost it with him, telling him he needed to 'butt the hell out' of her life now that she's an adult and that she didn't 'need his bloody advice'.

To which he replied, 'Okay then, I guess that means you don't need my money either. I'm stopping your allowance.'

Even though all the blood seemed to drain from her face, she said, 'Fine. I don't want anything from you any more anyway,' before she stormed off.

But despite the torrent of tears I found her in later, this change in circumstances seems to have lit something inside her.

So, I was delighted for her when she managed to land a well-paid job as an events and marketing manager at a new boutique hotel near Frome, which is about half an hour's drive south of Bath.

I've never seen her so relieved about something, especially when our hard-as-nails father made a point of calling to tell her how proud he was of her for securing it. As I well know, getting any kind of recognition out of him is a tough task.

When Dee told me he'd contacted her, I could tell by the emotion in her voice it meant the world to finally get some credit from him. You see, deep down – once you get past the blustery bravado – she's actually quite an insecure person with a gentle soul. She's had the rough end of the stick from our father since she was little and she's been desperate to prove him wrong about her lack of decisiveness and control over the direction of her life.

Which is funny because I want to prove him right about the things he says about me: that I'm built to run my own company and to be as successful as he is.

Like I say, it's a lot to live up to, but I'm down for it.

Just as I'm thinking this, my business partner, Jem, appears in our office.

Well, when I say 'office', I actually mean a basement room in a town house that my father bought recently and is allowing me to live in rent-free while it's being turned into individual flats. The deal is that I take in any out-of-hours deliveries, liaise with the project manager when he can't get hold of my dad and make sure the place looks lived-in to deter potential squatters and thieves. They're patently trumped-up excuses so my dad can feel he's supporting me in some way, since I've out and out refused to take a loan from him for my fledgling business. But this way, we can both pretend we're helping each other out without it feeling loaded.

I'm staying in the already converted garden flat, which consists of a kitchen-diner, a bathroom, a bedroom and the aforementioned living room that's doubling as the office, which we've been able to squeeze two desks into.

You see, Jem and I aren't quite at the stage where we can afford to pay rent for proper office space yet – or to pay ourselves wages – but we're working on it.

Getting a start-up business off the ground is really hard – harder than I'd ever imagined – and less fun than I'd thought it would be too, but both Jem and I are fully committed to making it work.

We've actually been good friends since the day we met during the first lecture of our degree course. I chose to sit next to him, thinking he looked like my kind of person with all his notes, books and stationery laid out neatly on the desk in front of him, and with an expression of focused attention on his face that reflected my own need to make the most of the three years ahead of me.

So, when he asked me to form this company with him, I jumped at the chance, even though business software wasn't exactly what I'd imagined choosing to develop for my first company. It could turn out to be a real money-maker though – and money is something Jem is going to need a lot of.

Thankfully, he's turning out to be a fantastic business partner: dedicated, smart and determined. The only thing that bothers me is that there's sometimes an odd, far-away look in his eye, and I'm never quite sure what he's thinking. He can be a bit of a closed book like that.

'Morning,' he says now, as he strides through the room and sits in his office chair, surveying his impeccably neat workstation and adjusting his keyboard so it lines up exactly with the edge of his desk. He does this every morning and this little ritual always makes me smile. I don't think he even realises he's doing it.

'Morning,' I reply. 'How was your weekend?'

'Yeah, good, thanks. I spent most of it coding.'

I shake my head at him. 'You're going to burn yourself out.'

He flips me a grin and his face lights up with it. He's a really attractive guy, though he doesn't seem to be aware of the fact. At least he doesn't act like he is.

I can't understand why he doesn't have women crawling all over him.

He's not mentioned having gone on any dates recently so I suspect he's thinking along the same lines as me: stay single and laser-focused until we've got this business off the ground.

I have wondered, on occasion, whether he's actually asexual because I don't remember him ever talking about a partner whilst at uni either. Though I suspect that was because he had a lot on his plate, what with managing the heavy workload of the course and also having to regularly travel back to the assisted living complex in Bath where his mum now lives, to deal with her increasing health needs.

Dementia is a horrific affliction, made doubly hard by the fact his dad passed away from a heart attack in Jem's second year and his mum gets confused and forgets that he died.

I can't imagine how hard all that must be for him to deal with. Not that he ever complains.

'Tea?' he asks me, already rising from his chair.

'Love one, thanks,' I say, running a hand through my hair and finding a couple of knots at the very end which I work free with my fingers. My hair is the physical feature I like most about myself. I've not cut it for years, barring the odd trim to neaten up split ends, and it hangs right down to the base of my spine now. I love the heavy weight of it across my shoulders. It's a bit like a comfort blanket, I guess.

I've managed to check through all the new emails that have appeared in my inbox since Friday – does everyone work at the weekends now? – before Jem returns with two mugs brimming with tea.

'Thanks,' I murmur, as he places one carefully next to my keyboard so as not to slosh any hot liquid onto my desk.

'Have we heard back about the funding round yet?' he asks hopefully, peering over my shoulder at my computer screen.

He smells like minty shower gel and fresh air.

I shake my head, pressing my mouth down at the corners. 'Not yet. But hopefully soon. When I chased it on Friday, they said they'll let us know by the end of this month.' I check the date on my watch. 'So in about two weeks' time.'

Jem nods. 'Okay.' He runs his hand over his jaw which, unusually, is covered in stubble this morning. 'God, I hope we get it. It'll be great to be able to start hiring so we can really get things off the ground. And start paying ourselves,' he adds.

I grimace. 'Yeah, I know what you mean. My savings are disappearing fast and I really don't want to have to ask my dad for a loan.'

Jem nods sagely. He knows all about the delicately balanced relationship I have with my father. They've met each other a few times now and to my amazement seem to get on pretty well, which is a real plus. The last thing I need is my dad on my back about the suitability of my business partner. Not that it's any of his business – and I intend to keep it that way.

Glancing down at my mobile, which is lying next to my keyboard, I see I have a message from my friend, Pete. Opening it up, I scan the text.

Hey, Bea. You're still in Bath, right? I know this is a long shot, but Jay's looking for a venue near you for his festival which is planned for next weekend (last minute, I know, but the place he booked just outside Bath has just had a nearby river break its banks and flood the grounds so camping there is impossible now). If you can think of anywhere he can approach, will you let me know? He's found somewhere available in Gloucestershire but they want an arm and a leg for it, which will just about bankrupt him. He's sold a lot of tickets though and doesn't want to let people down this late in the day, especially not after all the work he's put into it. He's in bits, poor thing. If you could pass this message on to anyone you can think might be able to help, we'd really appreciate it.

Love ya!

I pull a face, feeling a huge amount of pity for Jay, who's worked really hard to get his festivals up and running over the last couple of years. I wonder whether the hotel where Dee is working might be able to help.

She'll be driving there right now though, in heavy traffic, and I don't want to distract her. Deciding to call her at lunchtime, I wrap my hand around the mug of tea Jem delivered to me, enjoying the heat against my palm, and I'm about to lift it to my mouth when my mobile rings. I glance at the caller ID and – speak of the Devil – I'm bemused to see Dee's name lit up on the screen.

Huh.

That's really strange. She never calls me this early in the morning. Since she started her new job at the hotel, she's been careful not to be late – something she's been fired for at previous jobs. In fact, she told me the other day that she's been leaving an hour early most mornings to be on the safe side.

I pick up my phone and accept the call, my heart beating a little faster as a strange sense of foreboding licks at the edges of my mind. We're not the type of twins that feel each other's emotions, like some claim to be able to do, but there's something about the timing of this call that's setting my nerves on edge.

'Hey, you. Everything okay?' I ask.

There's a short pause, then the sound of my sister drawing in a raspy breath.

Uh oh.

'Um. Not really,' she says in a small, shaky-sounding voice.

My whole body goes on high alert, blood pumping hard through my veins.

'What's wrong?'

'I... er. I've hurt my ankle.'

'Okay,' I say, crossing my fingers that she's not underplaying this only to lead me in gently to the true horror of her injury. I'm ashamed to say that I'm not good with physical wounds, as she well knows. The sight of them does something weird to me, sending my blood sugar through the floor and on occasion making me faint.

It's my fatal flaw.

In all other respects, I'm a very practical person. But not with things like this.

I can already feel myself starting to sweat.

'It's a bit embarrassing actually,' she says, in an unusually discomfited voice. This isn't like Dee at all. She's normally full of bluster, even in the most trying of circumstances.

'What happened?' I ask tentatively.

'Well, the thing is, I bought some new shoes at the weekend

and they have a bit more of a heel on them than I'm used to,' she says in a more conversational tone now.

I begin to relax, reassuring myself she wouldn't be launching into one of her stories if she was lying broken on the floor.

'I thought they'd make me look more professional, you know, at my job. I want my boss to think I'm one of those powerful, intimidating women that Dad's always dating.' I'm reminded of the rapt look on her face when she described her new employer to me the other day. He's the son of a famous rock star and a well-known musician himself – a guitarist, I think – though I couldn't name one of his band's songs right now. I don't think they released many before they imploded. From what little I know about him, he led a pretty wild celebrity lifestyle – drink and drugs, the usual nonsense – and ended up being booted out of the band for not turning up for gigs.

Apparently, he went from being well respected to utterly disdained for being an over-privileged nepo baby in the space of about a year. And now he's using his family's wealth and connections to front the boutique hotel that Dee landed her job at and is proving to be a pretty *testing* boss. Whatever that means.

'Okay, but I think it'll take more than a pair of six-inch heels to make that a reality,' I say a little impatiently, wishing she'd get to the point.

I glance up to see Jem is looking over at me with a concerned frown on his face. I smile and mouth, 'It's just Dee,' to reassure him there's no real problem here.

He nods and looks back at his screen. He's met Dee a few times, so he knows exactly what I mean by that.

'Anyway,' she says, seeming to sense my frustration. 'I was on my way out to the car and my ankle went over when I was coming down the stairs.'

'You walked down those narrow stairs in new high heels?' I say, unable to keep the exasperation out of my voice.

'I know, I know, but I wanted to make sure I could manage stairs in them before wearing them around the hotel all day.' Her voice is shaky again now, like she's on the brink of tears.

Empathy shoots through me. I really should be kinder to her; she's trying hard to make this new opportunity work out and she doesn't need me criticising her too.

'How bad is it? Can you walk?' I ask.

She lets out a long sigh. 'See, that's the problem. I don't think I can. My ankle's blown up like a balloon and it's too painful to put any weight on it. I had to hop to the car in my bare feet – well, foot – but I don't think it's safe for me to drive.'

I shake my head and grimace at my desk, glad she can't see me right now. How does she manage to get into these scrapes all the time? It's baffling to me.

'Bea?' she says in a querulous voice into the silence.

And I know exactly what's coming next. I can see the rest of my day disappearing in a blur of hours sitting in an uncomfortable plastic chair, drinking bitter-tasting, watery instant coffee in the waiting room of the A&E department.

But to my surprise, she doesn't ask me to take her to the hospital.

Instead, she says, 'I need you to save my life and pretend to be me.'

2

DELILAH

Okay, when I said, 'I need you to save my life,' to my sister, I didn't mean that literally, of course.

What I was actually asking was if Bea could step in and help protect my fledgling career and potential relationship with the guy I can picture myself marrying one day.

So, no real pressure then.

'I know it's a huge ask,' I say to her when she arrives a few minutes after we end our call and gets into my car, where I'm still sitting, trying not to panic about what this injury could mean.

'It's more than huge, Dee.'

I give my sister a beseeching smile. She's such a good person and I hate to take advantage of her kindness, but I swear I wouldn't ask this of her if it wasn't incredibly important to me. I feel like I'm finally getting somewhere and I'm desperate not to mess it up now.

'This job could be – probably *will* be – the springboard to the rest of my life. It feels like a turning point. I'm not like you, Bea; I don't have the smarts and qualifications to aim for a high-flying career that'll pay off my student loans. I was lucky to get this job:

right place at the right time,' I lie, willing my face not to show it. 'I'll never get the opportunity of a position like this one again with my current meagre job experience in temping and cleaning. This role actually pays me a wage I can live on and it'll give me something impressive to put on my CV in case I don't manage to make it as an artist. It's an amazing opportunity for me; you get that, right?' I plead.

She's not looking at me, just staring at the dashboard in front of her.

I turn to fully face her and put my hands together in a prayer-like gesture. 'All I'm asking is that you turn up to my work today and make sure nothing goes wrong with the corporate event we're hosting. It should be really straightforward. It's just,' I take a steadying breath, 'it's for one of my boss's friends, so it has to go smoothly. At least, he's made it very clear that it needs to.'

Bea shoots me a look of deep concern, her brow furrowed.

'What do you mean? Is your job in jeopardy?'

My anxiety intensifies. I can't believe I'm dragging her into another one of my messes.

Why do these things always happen to me?

I lower my hands to my lap and link my fingers together to stop them visibly trembling. 'Um, well, yes, kind of. There's actually something I didn't tell you,' I say, the shame I've been keeping locked down for the last few days starting to trickle through me like ice water through my veins.

'The thing is,' I take another breath, 'I was so determined to get the position, I kind of stretched the truth a little about my suitability for it. I... er... might have used your qualifications as inspiration... a little bit.' I clear my throat, then rush on before Bea has a chance to say anything. 'I thought I'd be fine learning on the job and that I could ask you for some pointers if I started to struggle.' I glance at her, then look quickly away when I see the look of horror on her face.

'Oh, Dee, seriously? You lied on your CV?' she says.

Heat rushes to my face. 'Okay, Golden Child, I know it wasn't a great move, but you don't need to take everything so seriously. Chill out a bit.'

She opens her mouth to protest, but I just barrel on, desperately trying to recover from my faux pas.

'And anyway, I didn't lie exactly. I just fluffed it up a little. Embellished a few details, but the bones of it are all me. Everyone does it. And I wanted that job so badly. I need to be able to prove to myself that I can take on a responsible role and stick with it this time.' I take a fortifying breath. 'And it could lead on to all kinds of opportunities, especially when I'm mixing with the type of people who can afford to come to the hotel. People who can pay proper money for art. I was hoping to persuade Jonah to let me hang some of my pictures in the rooms with a view to selling them to guests. It's all about getting your work under the right noses. I have a whole plan worked out. It's a real win-win. I could paint and also be paid a good living wage from doing this job, just till I've made a name for myself. Trouble is, I've made a couple of rookie mistakes so I'm on a final warning. I swear though, Bea, they were only tiny things. He's a real perfectionist. I've been doing better in the last few days, but this will be the last straw for him.'

She blinks at me, looking baffled by this. 'Surely you can tell him you had an accident and you need to get checked out at the hospital though. He's got to understand that.'

I feel hot and panicky at the thought of how that conversation would go. 'I very much doubt it. I'm really not his favourite person at the moment and I'm worried he'll use this as an excuse for me not to pass my probation period if I don't turn up today.'

The exasperated huff she lets out tells me she's not *entirely* on board yet. Clearly, I need to lay it on the line for her, no matter how humiliating it is for me to admit it out loud.

'Please, Bea. It meant so much to me when Dad finally said, "Well done," to me for getting this job. I need to keep it so I don't have to go to him, cap in hand, and tell him that I failed and that he was wrong to be proud of me,' I say. 'That I'm the failure he always suspected I'd be and that I need his hand-outs after all.'

A shiver runs through me at the very idea of this and I feel the tears I've been keeping at bay for the last couple of months start to press dangerously at the back of my eyes.

Seeing me on the brink of a breakdown seems to get through to her because she reaches over and pulls me against her body, wrapping her arms around me.

'I know. I get it. He can be a real tyrant, but he just wants the best for you,' she whispers into my hair.

I nod against her shoulder, but her kindness, along with the shock of my accident and the residual savage ache it's left in my ankle all culminate in a wave of sorrow and frustration so strong, I let out an involuntary, loud sob.

'Oh, Dee, don't cry,' she says, leaning back and using her thumbs to wipe away the tears that are now cascading down my cheeks.

'I've... been trying... so hard,' I say to her, in a broken voice, between sobs, 'but no matter what I do, it's never enough. I'm not like you, Bea. Something always bloody trips me up!'

'I know, I know,' she soothes. She's an amazing sister, even if she does drive me crazy with her perfection some days. In fact, I'd probably hate her if she wasn't such a lovely human being.

'Okay,' she says, giving me a reassuring smile. 'I'll go to the hotel for you today and make sure everything goes smoothly, but you'll need to give me a full run-down of what to expect and be available on the phone if I have any questions. Okay?'

Pulling her back, hard against me, I wrap my arms tightly around her, relief flooding through me. I try not to feel bad about the tense way she's holding herself now.

'Thank you! Thank you!' I whisper, leaning back to look her in the eye. 'I'll make it up to you somehow, I swear.'

My sister smiles at me, but I can tell from her expression that she can't think of any way in which she'll ever need my help. Her life is too organised for that. She'd never be put on a warning for anything.

Untangling herself from me, she slaps her hands onto her knees. 'Right. I'm going to drive you to the hospital so you can get your ankle checked. You can tell me what needs to happen today on the way there. Then I'll nip back to your flat and borrow some of your clothes so no-one will turn a hair when I walk in as you.'

Something occurs to me when I hear the word 'hair'. 'Uh, Bea. What are you going to do about your hair?' I gesture to my chin length bob, then to her long swathe of locks.

Her eyes widen and her face seems to pale a little at this complication. 'Ah. Yeah. I'd not thought about that. I'll have to pretend I'm wearing a wig, or tuck it in or something.'

The scepticism I feel must show on my face though because her cheeks flush and the expression in her eyes turns a little wild.

'Don't worry about that now,' she says. 'I'll figure something out.'

I push away the surge of guilt I feel about putting her out like this. I know she'll find the perfect way to deal with everything though. It's her God-given gift.

'Thanks, Bea. You're a superstar. I love you. You know that, right?'

She just nods once, then puts her hand out for my car key, which I pass to her. 'I know. I love you too.'

This time, the reassuring hug she pulls me in for is full of the warmth I crave.

I breathe in the familiar, sweet scent of her. My lovely sister. My rock. She smells like home and comfort. Sanctuary.

What would I do without her?

Pulling away, she looks me right in the eye, the practical Bea fully back in evidence. 'Don't worry. It's going to be fine,' she says.

I swallow hard.

Bea's very rarely wrong about anything and I silently pray that this time isn't going to prove to be the exception to the rule.

3

BEATRICE

Even though I feel a strong sisterly duty to help Dee with her latest disaster, my heart sinks at the thought of having to explain this to Jem and ask if he minds if I have a day – or maybe a few days, depending on the extent of Dee's injury – away from running the business.

We'd made a commitment to each other to be entirely focused on getting it off the ground and had agreed not to have any time off until we were going strong.

I can't believe I'm having to renege on that promise already.

But Dee's family.

And she's always had the toughest time out of both of us, being the more emotionally sensitive one. Plus, the way our dad has always seemed to favour me hasn't helped, especially as our mum has been a pretty absent parent for the most part. She's far too self-involved. You can't ever rely on her to show up for you when you need her.

Even though Dee's pretended, for the most part, that she doesn't care about this inequality, I've always felt it as an invisible barrier between us.

When we were younger, I was always so grateful not to be in the firing line of our dad's wrath, I let her take the brunt of it.

And the guilt's weighed heavily on me over the years.

So, I feel like it's the least I can do to help her out with this situation.

At least it's not the worst time I could be asking this favour of Jem. We're in a bit of a holding pattern until we hear whether we've been successful with the funding we've applied for anyway, so it won't be the end of the world if I take a bit of time off right now.

But still, it feels like a big ask.

I really don't want him thinking I'm not fully on board with what we're trying to achieve.

My professional pride is at stake here.

So, after being briefed by Dee, dropping her at the hospital, then rushing back to her flat to borrow some of her clothes, I finally make it back to my place and search out Jem, who's sitting at his computer, hammering away at his keyboard. It always fascinates me to watch him work. He's the fastest typist I've ever seen; his fingers seeming to move without conscious thought as he writes the code we need for the financial accounts management system we're building.

'How is she?' he asks dryly, not looking away from his screen as he finishes off a line of code.

'She's at the hospital waiting for an x-ray of her ankle,' I say, perching carefully on the edge of my desk and waiting till he looks up at me. 'It's probably a bad sprain, but there's a chance she's broken a bone. I suspect she's going to be out of action for a while.'

'When you say, "out of action"—?' I can tell from his expression that he's already anticipated my need for some kind of goodwill here.

The problem is, Jem and Dee have never really got on that well. I wouldn't go so far as to say they're sworn enemies, but they don't seem to be able to be in the same room together without riling each other up. Their personalities are so different and it can make for an explosive mix whenever they're in the same vicinity.

So I'm not entirely sure how he's going to take this.

'I'm really sorry to ask, but can I have a couple of days off till we know how this is going to affect her?'

His sigh is heavy and I can tell he's struggling not to just snap a 'no' at me.

'What exactly has she got you to agree to do?' he asks instead.

It amazes me how intuitive he is some days.

'I'm just going to stand in for her at her job today so she doesn't get fired on the spot. Her new boss is a real piece of work from the sounds of it.'

He shoots me a look of confusion. 'Hang on a second. Do you mean you're going to pretend to be her?'

My face heats. 'Just for today, yes. There's an important event happening, apparently, and she's desperate not to let her boss down.' I hold up both hands at his expression of incredulity. 'I know, I know, but she's been trying so hard recently and this job is such a good opportunity for her.'

'You know you really can't hold yourself responsible for other people's happiness,' he says with a frown. 'And by "other people", I'm obviously talking about Delilah.'

'I know, but she got a rougher deal than me after our parents' divorce and it's taking her longer to figure out her life plan. Our mum's been next to useless about helping her make decisions about her future and there's no way she'd ask our dad for help. She just needs a break.'

His frown deepens. 'I'm not sure that's true. She seems to

have done perfectly well for herself so far with very little effort expended.'

I wave a hand at him, dismissing his concern. This same conversation has happened a few times recently – any time he suggests Dee is taking the piss in fact, which is often. 'Anyway, I've told her I'll do it.'

There's a heavy pause, then to my relief, he huffs out a sigh, then raises a hand in what looks like acquiescence. 'Fine. I guess it's not my place to comment on the state of your relationship with your sister.' He pauses, then clearly can't help adding, 'But it drives me crazy to see how much Dee plays on your sense of sisterly duty. I never see her doing the same for you.'

'No. Well, luckily I don't tend to need her help with anything.'

'Exactly,' he says, 'and I'm not sure how much you're actually helping her by trying to fix her messes for her. She needs to grow up and start taking responsibility for her own mistakes.'

'Give her a break, Jem. The sprained ankle wasn't her fault. It was an accident.'

He makes a non-committal sound in the back of his throat, then murmurs, 'If she wasn't so hung up on trying to shag her celebrity boss, it probably wouldn't have happened.'

I choose to ignore this, mostly because I know, deep down, that he's not wrong. You see, Jem and I overheard her the other day talking on her phone to a friend about how gorgeous both the hotel and her boss are. She's clearly fascinated by him, despite his bad boy reputation – or maybe because of it. Fame has always captivated Dee. I think there was some sort of scandal involving him recently, which was doing the rounds on social media a few months ago and only added to his troublemaker rep, but I didn't pay enough attention to be able to relate the ins and outs of it.

And I don't have time to form further defence of my sister right now either. I'm already running late for her job as it is.

'Please, Jem. Be kind. She's struggled with her mental health recently and she was crying on me earlier.'

I see his body language change as my words appear to have an impact on him. I use this to press my advantage. 'I swear I won't let this affect the business.' I cross my fingers in my lap, hoping to God my sister's actions won't make a liar out of me.

'Fine. Go and do her job for her. All I'm saying is, keep in mind you've got your own life to live. You can't live hers too.'

'I know. I hear what you're saying. Thanks, Jem. Seriously. I really appreciate your understanding,' I say, a mixture of relief and apprehension rushing through me.

I stand up and make for the door, feeling the lack of time pressing in on me.

I don't look back at Jem as I leave. I daren't.

In the car, I smooth down the skirt belonging to Dee that I've already changed into, trying to squash my nerves into a manageable low hum.

She assured me that I'll probably not even see Jonah Jacobson today. She thinks he'll be too busy hanging out with his friend, whose event it is, to notice me busying about behind the scenes.

But I don't have time to worry about that right now. I need to get going.

So instead, I take a breath and mentally cross everything that she's right and I'm not about to walk headlong into a disaster of my own.

4

JONAH

She's late.

Which is really bloody frustrating.

This is the one thing she promised me would never happen. But it appears I've been taken for a fool by a woman who had me convinced she just needed one more chance to show she was taking her role here seriously, despite a voice in the back of my head telling me not to believe a word she said.

What the hell is wrong with me? You'd think after the humiliating shitshow I went through with Tessa, I'd have learnt my lesson about trusting the things women tell me.

I'm ashamed to say that in my desperation to get the position filled quickly and things back on track after Tessa left, I only glanced at Delilah's CV before I met her at the interview and didn't follow up on her references. When she turned up, confidently promising she'd do a stellar job, I just hired her on the spot. She has a knockout smile and that day, I just needed someone around who had both positivity and agency.

I've regretted it since though.

The way she full-on flirts with me, not to mention the *incident* the other day, makes me think she's intent on securing more than just a job here.

But I can't have a relationship with my events manager. It would be way too tacky. People are bound to see it as a desperate move to even things up with my ex.

They already think I'm a massive loser after that bloody meme went viral.

Anyway, there's no way I'm launching into anything new so soon after what happened with Tessa. Mixing business and pleasure is a sure-fire way to implode your life – I'm living proof of that.

But I can't think about that right now.

I have a job to do.

This investor meeting we're hosting for my friend, Harry, today needs to go without a hitch. It's not only vital he comes out looking good, especially after all the support he's given me in the last year, but it's imperative for my own self-worth: to prove to myself I'm capable of successfully running things here on my own.

Unfortunately, today that involves Delilah pulling her finger out and making sure nothing goes wrong – as everything else under her supervision seems to have done so far. It's not been too much of a problem up to this point as they've only been small events and easy fixes, but if she doesn't do a good job today, she's going to have to go. No matter how much work that'll make for me in the short term.

I have to be able to trust my staff.

Just as I'm thinking this, I see her car coming down the drive and pulling into the staff car park.

Finally.

I watch her as she gets out. Her movements seem a little rushed and panicky, as if she's afraid I'm watching out for her. I'm guessing she's hoping I won't notice her late entrance though and just breeze in here in her usual carefree way.

Despite my irritation, I can't help but admire her long-legged, graceful gait as she makes for the staff entrance to the hotel that will bring her right past my office door. She's a snappy dresser and today she's wearing a slim, pencil skirt and a fitted leather jacket with a long, chunky scarf draped round her neck.

She's an attractive woman all right, with her big, blue eyes and wide, cupid-bow mouth.

Before the fucked-up events of a few months ago, I'd have found her increasingly unsubtle advances both entertaining and charming, but I'm well past that point now. They just remind me of what an idiot I was to have been so trusting of Tessa. In retrospect, I realise I let her beauty and charisma dazzle me to the point where I missed what was going on right under my nose.

I'm never letting myself fall for that bullshit again.

There's a bang as Delilah lets the outside door to the staff area shut behind her and I stroll out from my office, folding my arms across my chest in readiness for the confrontation.

'Morning, Delilah. Good of you to finally join us,' I say.

Okay, so it's not my wittiest retort ever, but I'm not in the mood for any nonsense today.

She comes to an abrupt halt when she sees me there, waiting for her.

'Oh!' she says, staring at me like she's seen a ghost, her eyes wide and a little wild. 'I wasn't expecting to see you this morning.'

Is she high?

Surely not. She knows how much the smooth running of this

event means to me – and that I'll fire her ass if anything goes wrong with it.

'You're late. You promised me you'd be on time.'

She visibly swallows. 'I... yes. You're absolutely right. I'm really sorry. There was some traffic. I think some animals got loose and were roaming—'

But I don't have the patience for her excuses and I hold up my hand in a halting gesture. 'Whatever. Just make sure everything else goes perfectly today.'

Her answering nod is firm, which makes me think she took the lecture I gave her on Friday, about the fine line she's treading at the moment, seriously.

Not that her continuing to work for me is guaranteed anyway. Things clearly need to change around here if I'm going to make this place a success.

'Okay, will do, Mr Jacobson.'

That's weird. She's never called me Mr Jacobson before. She usually just calls me, 'Boss,' in that teasing way of hers.

In fact, now I look at her properly, there's definitely something slightly off-kilter about her. Not bad off-kilter though, just... she's giving me a different vibe to the one I usually get from her.

What the hell is it that's bothering me?

'You seem different. What's different about you?' I snap. The need for everything to go smoothly today is clearly fraying my nerves.

'Er, my hair maybe? I fancied having long hair today so I'm wearing a wig.' She flashes me a smile but her eyes don't quite meet mine. What's she playing at? There's something not right here.

'Well, for God's sake, take it off. This isn't fashion week. I need you focused on being professional and making sure this meeting runs like clockwork, not disappearing off to the ladies' every five minutes to pimp your appearance.'

Her eyes narrow a fraction before she readjusts her expression to one of consolatory cheerfulness. 'I'll tie it up out of the way.'

I sigh. 'No. I said take it off. If you fight me on this, you can consider yourself fired.'

I won't have it, this obsession with appearance. It's an unnecessary distraction. And I've had enough of her trying to get round me with her flirty ways. She's here to do a job.

She appears a little shaken by my demand, her hands shooting up to her hair as if she's afraid I'll whip the wig off her head right there in the corridor, and I experience a sting of self-reproach. But I'm not going to pander to her whims right now, not when Harry's due to arrive at any moment.

Colour rises in her cheeks.

'The thing is, I let a student hairdresser cut my hair at the weekend and she made a bit of a mess of it. I didn't have the heart to ask her to fix it. That's really why I'm wearing a wig.'

This small act of humility does something to my insides. Delilah's never struck me as the compassionate type. She seems a little too self-centred for that.

I guess it goes to show that you shouldn't judge people before you get to know them – something I've deliberately been avoiding doing with Delilah since she started here. It seemed too risky, considering the way she looks at me from under her lashes with such intensity, like she's sizing me up for a fling.

Despite my annoyance with her, I feel my skin prickle at the thought of it. It's been a while since I had sex and the lack of it is clearly getting to me.

My gaze drops to that perfect cupid's bow on her top lip. It's so pretty, I want to run my finger over the undulations of it. But I know where that could eventually lead and that's the last thing I should be getting into.

Huh. That's strange. There's a small, faint scar on her top lip, just to the right of the bow, that I've never noticed before. Not that I've spent a lot of time looking at her mouth. Or at least, I've tried not to. And I really shouldn't be doing it now. She might read more into it than just idle curiosity.

Glancing back up, my gaze locks with hers and a strange connection seems to pass between us, like the air's alive with the potential for something wholly improper to happen here. She's staring back at me as if she's thinking the same thing I am.

My heartbeat picks up its pace and I feel it thudding in my chest.

Ah hell. This isn't good. I really need to kill this. Right now.

'Okay, fine. Keep it on today, but I want it gone by tomorrow. Is everything set for this morning?' I ask, to distract myself from my wayward thoughts.

She seems to snap to attention at my question and raises a folder she's had tucked under her arm. 'I think so, yes. I'm just going to go over everything to make sure.'

'Good,' I say, then turn and get out of there, away from her unnerving presence and the inappropriate impulses she's teasing from me.

This event's in her hands now so I should leave her to it.

I head back to the reception desk to check whether Harry's arrived yet, my blood still pulsing hard through my veins.

Just as I'm walking into reception, I see the heavy oak front door swing open and Harry comes striding in.

'Hey, man,' he says, giving me a salute. 'How's it going? Are we all set?'

'Yeah, good. We're ready,' I say, going over to clap him on the back, hoping to God that Delilah isn't going to make me look like an idiot today.

'Cool, I'll head to the room and get my laptop set up with your projector then. The team should be arriving in fifteen.'

'No problem. Delilah should be here in a minute, ready to greet them.'

'Ah, the lovely Delilah,' Harry says, his voice heavy with meaning. He met her briefly last week and seemed pretty taken with her. He even went so far as to suggest she might be a good distraction for me, since I've totally failed to get back in the dating game, like he's been urging me to do.

Harry never really took to Tessa, so he wasn't entirely surprised, or concerned, when she took off.

I wait till Harry heads off to the room we're using to host his investor's meeting in today, then walk out of the main hotel doors for a breath of air.

Turning back to survey the building, I feel the usual rush of affection for the impressive, honey-coloured, stone-fronted grandeur of the house.

Gladbrooke House is a Grade I listed Georgian country manor, surrounded by a hundred acres of fields and woodland just south of Bath, and the place I most feel at home. There's something about it that makes me feel happy to be here. It has such a warm, comforting air. Despite the neglect it's seen, it still feels as though it's hosted a lot of happy memories throughout its existence.

My father bought the place in the noughties in order to 'diversify his portfolio'.

The previous owner had been pummelled by inheritance tax and had totally let the place go, before reluctantly selling up, so it was in a real state for a number of years.

My dad brought in a team of people to bring it back to life

from the broken-down wreck it had been, but he didn't spend the money on it that it really needed. So it just sat there, unloved for most months of the year while he was off performing on his international tours.

Since my brother and I were at boarding school from the age of seven, we only got to visit here sporadically during the holidays when we were young. My mum and dad never married and they split up when I was eight, so after that, I came here less than half the time, spending the rest of it in London with Mum and her new partner, or in one of my dad's other homes around the world. I've always loved the place though and during the breaks from university, I used to invite friends to come and stay and we'd have wild parties here.

Good times.

Last year, after my stint in rehab, my dad offered it to me as a bolthole till I was back on my feet. He'd been intending to put the place on the market but hadn't quite got round to it. He has very little attention these days for anything other than playing with his band or living a sun-drenched, booze-soaked life on the Italian coast with his fitness-obsessed new wife.

Rock stars. What a charmed life they live.

I'd thought for a while that that's what I wanted from my life too, but when it came down to it, it turned out I wasn't cut out for it. The expectation that I'd be as successful as my old man weighed heavy on me.

From the outside, it must have looked like I'd got everything I wanted in life – but in reality, it didn't feel like that.

As an unconscious response, I let myself get sucked into the partying lifestyle around it and ended up turning to booze and drugs to prop me up and turn off the fear and self-loathing I felt.

Which led to me completely losing the plot, my career and any kind of status I'd worked to achieve.

So that's how I ended up here, keeping a low profile and trying to make a fresh start in a new profession.

I'm determined to make my own mark on the world now, independent of my dad's fame.

I've persuaded him to let me run the place as a boutique hotel for a year, partly so we could keep the house that means more to me than any other in the family, but also because I was struggling with what to do with myself at that point after my music career hit a brick wall. For once, he didn't give me any shit about the sorry state of my existence and gracefully agreed to let me 'do my best' with it.

I have six months left to prove I can make a success of it as a business so I can apply for a loan to buy the place off him.

To prove to everyone that I can stand on my own two feet.

That I'm not the waste of space some people have me pegged as.

I've devised some grand plans for moving the business forward, now I'm in the right mindset to take them on, some of which have had to go on the backburner for now. I'm hoping Dee will be able to help me bring them to fruition, now that Tessa's fucked off.

It was meant to be the two of us doing this together, but that's never going to happen now.

Despite her initial reluctance to leave London and move here, I'd thought Tessa had seemed to come round to the idea of running the hotel with me.

When we first opened to the public, we offered bed and breakfast accommodation in five of the twenty rooms, which we'd updated to luxury standard, thanks to the money I raised from selling my flat in London. The rest of them still need a lot of money spending on them to bring them up to scratch though, which I was hoping to fund through profits, so they're an ongoing project.

The whole enterprise was much more of a slog than either of us had anticipated.

A marriage wrecker – if we'd actually got married, like we'd planned to.

Trouble was, I didn't want to use my fame to bring in business, so I kept a low profile, leaving Tessa to be the face of the hotel. But it turned out that people coming to stay were there to try and catch sight of me – and the fucked-up mess I was after becoming such a social pariah – which frustrated both them and Tessa.

I wasn't in any kind of state to face the judgemental stares of strangers though and once word got out that I was nowhere to be seen, visitor numbers and bookings started to dwindle.

This didn't sit well with Tessa at all.

I run a hand over my face, trying to dispel the tension that always pops up whenever I think about how our relationship imploded.

Those first weeks after she left are a total blur now. I spent most of the time drunk. But after Harry's take-no-prisoners intervention, I managed to get my shit together. Not that I haven't thought about reaching for the bottle pretty much every morning since. But I promised him I'd not rely on the demon booze to get through my days any more.

And I, at least, am a person of my word.

Trouble is, it's now become clear that running things here single-handedly isn't going to be as straightforward as I'd imagined.

I'd thought word of mouth would be enough to get new business in, but it seems I can't rely on that to bring in enough regular revenue in low season. So I now need to consider whether it's worth the stress and hassle to keep the place going and I'm feeling the pressure of only having six months left to prove that either way.

The sound of a car coming up the long, tree-lined driveway towards the house distracts me from my thoughts and I turn around to see that Harry's associates are starting to arrive.

Okay then, here we go. Show time.

5

BEATRICE

My, oh my, oh my, oh my.

What a stressful day this is turning out to be.

I had no idea Dee's role here was so intense. I can see now why she didn't think she'd be able to do it with an injured ankle.

I'm exhausted and very much looking forward to getting home for a rest, but I still have another hour to go.

All morning I was back and forth to the conference room, making sure they had everything they needed set up for their presentations, which involved rebooting the Wi-Fi and trying about fifty different cables to get their laptop to connect to the projector. Then I got caught up with checking that the drink and lunch orders were correct and were being delivered at the right time by the catering staff, who I had to pretend I'd already met and was friendly with, which got a bit sticky when I couldn't remember what anybody's name was. I just ended up calling them, 'Lovely' or, 'Mate', which was just plain weird because, unlike Dee, I never use terms of endearment.

Then, as soon as Jonah's friend appeared not to need me any more, I sat down to check through a massive list of emails that seem to have been waiting, unopened, in Dee's inbox for the last week. Not to mention the time I spent looking over the woefully inadequate marketing plan she's been putting together to get some much-needed new business into the hotel.

She's really not on top of it at all. It's clear from the number of chasing messages, unpaid invoices and unanswered queries I've been reading through that she's dropping the ball all over the place. My sister is a smart cookie in lots of ways – even though academia never suited her – and incredibly creative, but this is clearly not a natural role for her to fill. Her main problem is she doesn't seem to have a system in place for handling any of it. It's all a bit slapdash. It's all a bit *Dee*.

After going to check on the delegates in the conference room and seeing that it's now empty of people, I flop back down into the office chair at Dee's desk and drop my head in my hands. I've not stopped, even for lunch, since walking through the door to the hotel this morning and bumping straight into Dee's grumpy boss.

Who is *scorching* hot.

I'd expected not to feel anything in particular for Jonah Jacobson, not being a fan of 'bad boys' and having very little interest in rock stars, who all seem to come with enormous egos and bad social habits. But I have to admit, there's something about the guy.

When Dee described him as 'fine as all get-out', I didn't pay that much attention. Her idea of attractive and mine usually rank on entirely different scales.

But not this time.

She was right on the money.

Not that I'd ever actually be interested in him as a partner. I have more sense than that. Men with a reputation like his are only ever interested in themselves.

And I'm here for a very specific purpose: to make sure Dee doesn't lose her job.

Speaking of which, there was an unnerving moment earlier, during that ridiculous back-and-forth about my 'wig', when I thought he'd rumbled me. He was staring at me with such a penetrating look in his eyes, I could have sworn he was reading my mind and was about to out me as a fraud.

But then it also felt like there was more subtext to that look as well. There was a strange, unnerving sort of connection between us, which made me wonder whether something less *professional* has been going on between him and my sister.

The idea of it – at least the notion of what it might be like to get cosy with him in that way – did something strange to my insides.

Which was extremely unsettling.

So, it was a relief when he snapped us out of the highly charged atmosphere by walking away, leaving me to get on with the job alone.

My legs had felt like jelly for a while after that and I spent the rest of the morning praying I wouldn't bump into him again.

The best thing would be for me not to have to see him before I leave this evening.

Just as I'm thinking this – as if he really *can* read my mind – Jonah walks through the door to my office and comes to a halt in front of my desk, his arms folded in front of him, making his tidy biceps bulge, and his face set in an expression of quizzical expectation.

'So?' he asks, 'how's everything going here?'

I swallow hard at the sight of him, then for some reason feel compelled to jump up from my seat and stand in front of him, as if I owe him this deference.

Or maybe I just feel self-conscious, staring up at him.

Because I didn't imagine it earlier; he's just as striking as I remember, with his deep-blue eyes and strong-jawed, heavy-browed appeal. There's something fierce about him too, which I guess is a trait he's inherited from his famously imperious father.

Undeniable charisma.

Unfortunately, I think my racing inner thoughts must be showing in my expression because he frowns at me and to my utter shock says, 'You're not going to try and kiss me again, are you?'

My mouth falls open and I stare at him in confusion, before quickly pulling myself together when I remember he thinks he's talking to my sister.

What the heck were you thinking, Dee?

'No, of course not,' I mumble, trying to force my expression into something that resembles jokey affront.

He frowns at my unconvincing response, then gives a small shake of his head, as if he thinks he's overstepped a line.

'Forget I said that,' he says, shifting on the spot. 'I shouldn't have brought it up again.'

What's going on here? I want to ask him. But I bite my lip.

Dee has got some serious explaining to do when I get home.

'Um. Okay,' is all I can manage. This is so awkward. I'm totally on the back foot and it's making me twitchy.

I see his Adam's apple bob up and down as he swallows and I momentarily wonder what his skin would smell like if I pressed my mouth against his neck there.

What's got into you, Bea! That's the last thing you should be thinking about right now – especially with this guy.

He doesn't seem to be aware of how much I'm spinning out though, thank goodness.

'Well, Harry tells me things went smoothly today, so I thought I'd come and say thanks for your hard work.'

I feel myself relax a little at that. So Dee's not getting fired today, at least.

Phew!

'My pleasure,' I say, with a smile.

He almost smiles back at me. But not quite.

'Actually, Delilah, I still need to talk to you about your position here, I'm afraid.'

Uh oh! Perhaps I relaxed too soon.

'What do you mean?' I ask, aware of a quaver invading my voice.

'I took a look at your marketing plans over the weekend.'

My stomach sinks. 'Ah.'

'We need to get more new business in over the low season and I don't think your current ideas are going to cut it.'

'Oh, I see, well, I—'

'You're going to have to do better than this to pass your probation.'

I can tell from the look on his face he's not expecting Dee to keep her job here for much longer.

My stomach lurches. I need to think of something fast.

'I know the marketing plan you saw isn't up to scratch, but I've only just started working on it so it's nowhere near ready. I have lots more ideas,' I say desperately.

I have to get Dee more time to pull things back. Now I know what's required of her, I can sit with her in the evenings and work up a new marketing plan, which could turn things around here.

A memory from this morning flashes into my head and it suddenly occurs to me that I might have the perfect solution – in the short term, at least.

'Actually,' I say, holding up a wait-a-second finger, 'speaking of opportunities, I was going to talk to you about this once Harry's event was over. A good friend of mine's partner, Jay, runs leave-no-trace festivals: Burning Man sort of style. They're incredibly popular, but he's struggled recently to find a suitable venue to hold them at. Most people camp, so he needs a lot of outdoor space. He texted me earlier to say the grounds of the place he booked for the next one, which is a few miles away from here, flooded recently and the new place he's considering moving it to is incredibly expensive. Seeing this place—' I shake my head, reminding myself I'm supposed to have been here for a few weeks. '*Knowing* this place better now, I think it would be perfect for it. I'm sure he'd jump at the chance to move it here if we offer it. Apparently, he's sold a lot of tickets and would be really grateful for a last-minute solution. It's supposed to go ahead this Thursday. It's a beat-the-winter-blues long weekend. I know it's short notice, but I don't think we have anything else booked in at the moment, not even any hotel guests.'

I suck in a long breath after I finish my monologue and look at him with hope swelling in my chest.

He continues to survey me with that intense stare of his and my stomach does another loop the loop.

'Hmm. It's not exactly the type of event I imagined we'd hold here,' he says, then looks away, frowning up at the ceiling, as if all his concerns are written up there.

'Jay's incredibly strict about protecting the location so you'll not even know the festival was here once it's been cleared away, I promise.'

'That's quite a promise to make, Dee,' he says with one eyebrow raised.

All I can think is *he called me Dee, not Delilah*, which I'm hoping means I'm – or rather Dee's – back in his good books.

My heart thuds hard as I wait to see if I've earnt my sister a reprieve.

Finally, he looks at me again and gives a curt nod. 'Okay. Let's give it a try. We don't exactly have a lot of other options right now anyway. Give your friend a call and see if we can come to an arrangement about cost.'

My whole body seems to sigh in relief and I feel my muscles begin to unknot.

'Okay. Thank you. I'll call him right now,' I say, sitting back down at my desk and pulling my mobile out of my pocket. I busy myself looking up Pete's number and when I glance back up, I realise Jonah is watching me with an intense, contemplative frown on his face.

I blink up at him, my skin rushing with tingles as the same unsettling feeling I felt under his gaze this morning washes over me again.

Before I can say anything else, he snaps his eyes away from mine and strides out of the room, leaving me sitting there staring after him, my whole body humming with a strange sort of tension.

I force the feeling down, then take a calming breath and tap on Pete's number, once again crossing my fingers for a good outcome.

* * *

An hour later, I pull Dee's car into a space right in front of my house and rush in on shaky legs, hoping to find my sister there to let her know about the – frankly pretty darn exciting – developments from the day.

I'm buzzing with adrenaline as I toe off my shoes and dash into my bedroom, finding her there, sprawled out on my bed. She's sitting up against the headboard with her right leg propped up on one of my pillows, her phone in her hand and a look of nervous expectation on her face.

It takes me less than five minutes to run her through the events of the day, her expression changing from worry to exultation as I tell her that Jonah was pleased with the way his friend's event went.

'Phew! Thank goodness,' she says, her voice light with relief. She sits up straighter and a flash of pain crosses her face as her swollen ankle shifts on the pillow.

'How is it?' I ask, realising in my excitement that I've not even checked about the outcome of the x-ray yet.

'It's not broken, but it's a bad sprain,' she says, her voice heavy with self-pity.

I force myself not to roll my eyes at her. She can be a real drama queen sometimes.

Not that I care too much at the moment. If she's not able to go back to work for a while, it means I'll be able to put my plan into action myself, which would be no bad thing since I already know how Jay's festivals work, having been to one of them. So I say, 'Sorry to hear that,' in my most soothing voice.

'I'm not sure how I'm going to get about. It hurts way too much to walk on it at the moment and it's throbbing with pain even when I'm sitting still. According to the doctor, it could be up to two weeks till the swelling's gone down and I'm able to walk around normally again.'

'Okay, well, don't worry. I can keep going in pretending to be you this week. So you can rest it for a few more days. Jonah didn't seem to suspect anything today, so I think we'll get away with it.'

I pause, considering how best to put what I need to tell her without worrying her too much. I decide to just go for it.

'The thing is, Dee, he was talking today about you not passing your probation unless you pull your socks up. There's quite a bit you've let slide and he's not overly impressed with your marketing plan.'

At the look of horror on her face, I hold up my hand, trying to reassure her. 'Don't panic. I think I might have negotiated a bit more time to turn things round. You know my friend, Pete? Well, his partner, Jay, needs a venue for his festival this coming weekend – the place he booked had some flooding in the grounds so it can't be used for camping – and I suggested we offer Gladbrooke House as a replacement venue, which both Pete and Jay thought was a great idea.' I pause to check her reaction to this, but she just nods slowly and waits for me to finish.

'It's a relatively small festival, more of a big fight-the-winter-blues party really, so totally manageable to have it there at short notice. Anyway, I was thinking, if you're not able to get around for a few days yet, perhaps I should keep doing your job till the festival's finished, then you can take over again. Jay's willing to pay a decent fee for the hire of the place, which seemed to satisfy Jonah. I think he'll be reluctant to let you go when you're bringing in business like that.'

'When *you're* bringing it in, you mean,' Dee corrects me.

My face heats. I'm not doing a great job of being subtle about it being an opportunity she wouldn't necessarily have converted and I'm worried I'm in danger of upsetting her. The last thing I want is for Dee to think I'm trying to muscle in on her job, but I'm actually quite excited about the idea of being involved in hosting the festival at the hotel now.

'I can help you with your marketing plans, if you like? For when you go back,' I say tentatively.

Dee's not looking at me now, but is staring down at her damaged ankle. 'Okay. That sounds like a plan. If you're really sure you don't mind doing that?'

'I just need to clear it with Jem, but otherwise, I'm good for it,' I reassure her.

Finally, she smiles again. 'Okay then. Let's go for it.'

I nod and try hard not to grin. It all feels like a bit of an adventure now, something I've not had in quite some time, and it's... enlivening.

'So how did you get away with your new hairstyle?' Dee asks, nodding at my hair, which I've had tied away from my face all day.

Ah, yes, of course. That was something I'd need to deal with if I'm going to keep stepping in for Dee.

My stomach turns over.

'I pretended I was wearing a wig to disguise a bad haircut.' I take a steadying breath, finding it incredibly hard to say the next words. 'But I'll need you to cut it off for me. There's no way I'll get away with playing on that story for the rest of the week.' I screw up my face. 'And maybe it's time for a change anyway?' I finish lamely.

'Really?' Dee says, apparently shocked by my suggestion.

'Yes,' I say, with conviction this time, fighting my jitters. 'Let's do it.'

It does seem like a good time for a change. I've been hanging on to my childhood hairstyle for too long now and it's probably time to try something new.

I'm not sure what's made me feel like this, but I'm just going to run with it for now.

'Ok-ay,' she says, clearly not convinced I'm entirely happy with the decision, but willing to go with it anyway. 'Grab the kitchen scissors and I'll chop it off for you.'

* * *

Fifteen minutes later, I'm holding my now detached ponytail in my hand and trying not to cry as I feel a breeze tickle the back of my neck. Dee's done a pretty good job of trimming it to make it as straight as possible, but I can still barely stand to look at myself in the mirror.

I look so different.

I look like Dee.

Oh, my beautiful hair.

I take a stuttering breath.

But it had to be done. And it'll grow back if I decide I don't want to keep it this short.

I reach up and tug at the freshly shorn ends, still in a state of shock about how different it feels.

My comfort blanket is gone.

All gone.

It'll be worth it, though, if it helps to even things up with my sister so I can stop feeling so guilty about the advantages I've had through getting preferential attention from my dad.

Dee, who's sitting behind me on the bed, shuffles forward and rests her chin on my shoulder. We both stare into the mirror at the double image.

'Hey, look, we're twins!' she says with a twinkle in her eye.

I can't help but laugh, even though I still want to cry a little bit.

'We're a couple of hotties, aren't we?' she says, when my face falls back into a slightly stricken expression.

I give her a weak smile this time.

'Speaking of hotties. What did you think of Jonah?' she asks, widening her eyes and waggling her eyebrows at me.

There's a weird little flutter in my stomach at the sound of his name.

Then I remember the attempted kiss.

'Ah, yes. I have a bone to pick with you. Were you ever going to tell me that you tried to snog your boss?' I ask, one eyebrow raised.

Dee bats her hand at me. 'Ah, that was just a misunderstanding,' she says, but the look in her eye is suspiciously shifty. 'I was just being extra friendly to try and shake him out of a bad mood and he took it the wrong way.'

'Hmm.' I'm not entirely convinced by this.

'You've met him; he's a total grump, right?' she says, screwing up her nose. 'A sexy grump, but very – what's the word? – cantankerous.'

'Hmm. I can see why you might say that.' I really don't want to get drawn into a discussion with Dee about how Jonah makes me feel. I'm not entirely sure I could describe it to her anyway.

'Mind you, I'd be grumpy too if I was most famous for being the Reverse Darcy,' she says.

I turn to face her, frowning in confusion. 'The what?'

'Reverse Darcy,' she repeats, as if I should know what that is.

'What's—?' I begin to ask, but I'm interrupted by a knock on the door. 'Come in,' I call.

Jem walks into the room. He stops abruptly when he sees the two of us, sitting side by side, looking at him expectantly.

'Whoa!' he says with alarm in his voice. 'What happened to your hair?'

I lift my fingers to the shorn ends, remembering all over again how we've just butchered it. To my horror, tears well in my eyes, but I quickly blink them back.

'Sorry, Bea, that was rude of me,' he says, with an apologetic grimace. 'It, er, looks nice.'

I have to give him credit for at least trying to sound convincing, even though he's way off the mark.

'Just trying something new,' I lie.

He nods, but doesn't press me further. 'Okay. Well, I'm going to head off. There's nothing I need to tell you from today. It's been quiet.'

'Oh, good. Yes. Sorry, I was about to come and check in with you.'

'No problem,' he says.

I realise he's not looked over and acknowledged Dee once since he came in. I hope she's not got in his way today.

I slide off the bed and stand up, gesturing for him to leave the room with me.

Once we're in the corridor, I turn to him and say, 'Thanks again for being so understanding about letting me have time off. Dee really appreciates it too.'

He frowns a little at that, but doesn't say anything.

'Her ankle is pretty badly damaged, it seems, so she's going to struggle to get into work this week.' I take a breath, then plunge straight in. 'Could I take the rest of the week off, do you think?' I wait with bated breath to see what his reaction is going to be to the request. It seems he's already anticipated I'll ask for this – again – and folds his arms, before giving me a reluctant-looking nod.

'I thought you might say that. Dee's already given me the full run-down on her *injury*.' He says this with a level of sarcasm I've never heard from him before. So I guess she has got in his way today then.

'I'm really sorry about all this, Jem.'

'Um-hm,' is all he says.

'Just this week, then I'll be back.'

'Yeah. Sure. Okay. I guess so. Not that you're giving me much choice.' He raises his eyebrows pointedly.

'You're a good friend, you know that?'

Finally, he smiles at me. 'Yeah. All right, there's no need to patronise me.'

I cuff his arm gently in jest. 'Seriously. Thank you.'

Again, he just nods. 'Well, anyway. I'm heading off. I'll see you next week then. Do you want me to check the builders don't need anything handling before I leave each evening, or will you be back in time to do that?'

The question makes another snag pop into my head. 'Actually, Dee's going to need to stay here for a little while, in my room, till she can climb all the stairs up to her attic flat again safely. It's probably easier if I stay at her place till she's mobile again. I'm sure it won't be for long. So she can do the check-ins and be on hand if they need anything.'

He visibly stiffens, then gives one last curt nod. But as he turns away, I could swear I catch him rolling his eyes heavenward.

I ignore it though, and the sinking feeling of apprehension. I can't worry about that right now.

Hopefully, Dee will keep well out of his way this week and I won't come back to find them at each other's throats.

The last thing I need is my sister and my best friend falling out with each other.

Things are complicated enough as it is.

6

JONAH

I'm pacing the floor of my office the next morning when Dee's car pulls into the car park with ten minutes to spare before her contracted start time.

I watch her hurry towards the hotel, her bobbed hair blowing in the gentle breeze.

At least she's not wearing that bloody wig again today.

But I still have a few choice words for her after the phone call I've just had to field.

As soon as she walks in through the door, the smile drops from her face when she sees me there waiting for her with my arms folded again. I beckon for her to follow me into my office and wait till she's sat down in the chair opposite me before launching into my rant.

'I've just had a really pissy call from a prospective customer who queried us about hiring the hotel for their wedding venue this summer over two weeks ago. Why the hell haven't you replied yet? We can't leave emails unanswered for that long. It makes us look like chumps who don't know what the hell they're doing!'

Her face seems to pale. 'I'm sorry, it must have got knocked off my email list by mistake.'

'That's not good enough! It's not like we're fully booked or anything. We need to get that kind of business in.'

She nods slowly, her eyes wide and worried.

I fight back a sting of discomfort at the thought that I'm being unnecessarily aggressive. But it's been one thing after another going wrong and my patience is wearing very thin now.

'You're absolutely right. I'll get onto them right away and offer my sincere apologies.'

I let out an exasperated sigh and stare up at the ceiling, trying to get my annoyance under control. I'm seriously on the cusp of firing her on the spot, but then what will I do? I really don't want to have to go through the time-consuming process of hiring for her role again.

'Don't worry, I'll fix it. And it won't happen again,' she says confidently now, looking me dead in the eye when our gazes lock again.

Can I let myself believe she really means that? It certainly seems like she does from the serious expression on her face.

Not that I have a lot of choice right now.

'Fine. Make sure you do.'

She nods and goes to stand up.

'And Dee?'

'Yes?'

'No more mistakes.'

She just nods again before turning and walking away.

A couple of hours later, I'm making myself a coffee in the kitchen when Dee strides over to me with a purposeful expression on her face.

'Okay, I called the prospective customer and apologised and gave them a couple of ideas about how we could best use the grounds and facilities here to stage their wedding. Apparently, the female partner is a big Agatha Christie fan, so I said we could orchestrate a 1920s-style reception with croquet and cocktails on the lawn and a pianist playing Cole Porter songs while they take photos by the gazebo, or maybe in front of the lake.'

A shiver of horror runs through me when I think of that place and the humiliation it's brought me.

She seems to notice my reticence because a flash of worry crosses her face. 'But if you don't think that's a good idea—'

I hold up a hand. 'No, no. It's a great idea.'

Confusion clouds her eyes, but I'm not about to go into my feelings about the lake with her right now. It's not like I'll need to go down there myself. She can take care of all of that.

'Oh! Okay, well, great,' she says, looking a little surprised at my inconsistency, but quickly putting on a professional face. 'Well, they seemed very keen and asked me to send over a quote so I'll go and get on with it then.'

'Good, you do that,' I say, noting a flicker of disappointment on her face that I hadn't been more effusive with my praise. But it's not a done deal yet. If she brings this business in, then I'll make sure she knows how pleased I am with her performance.

* * *

For the next couple of days, Dee makes an effort to not only to be on time each morning, but early. So early, in fact, I miss her coming into the building and have to search her out in the hotel or the grounds where she always seems to be on the phone to the festival organiser, Jay.

There are a tense couple of hours where we're not sure we have all the right licences to hold a festival at the hotel, but Dee takes charge of this, calling a friend of hers from uni who's now a qualified solicitor.

'I pulled in a bit of a favour and she's looked over all the documentation. It seems we're fine and don't need to apply for a temporary event notice in this instance, which is helpful because we'd be out of time to do it at this late notice,' she tells me with a huge grin.

Her relief is palpable and I almost smile back at her.

But I can't quite bring myself to trust she has everything in hand yet, so I just nod.

She seems a little disappointed at my lukewarm response, but I remind myself I'm her boss, not her friend.

I have to admit though, I'm a bit taken aback by how much more organised she appears to be now as she gets the place ready for this event. For the first time since she started, she actually seems excited about the job she's doing and it's given her a spring in her step.

Not that she was exactly morose before.

But it's odd though.

The more I watch her work – whilst trying not to be too blatant about checking up on what she's doing – the more I feel like I've actually got her completely wrong up till now.

Which is weird.

There's definitely something different about her, but I can't put my finger on exactly what it is. Physically, she looks the same, I think. Unless it's something to do with her hair? She seems to touch it all the time now. Perhaps she's paranoid it still looks bad after her disastrous haircut the other day. But I don't think that's it. At least, it looks okay to me.

No. It's a feeling I get from her. A vibe that wasn't there before.

Perhaps it's because I've finally seen her take some initiative and show me she really can be as good at her job as she initially promised.

What do they call that?

Competency porn.

I've always found skills more attractive than looks.

Yeah, that must be it.

Because she's definitely proved herself to be up to the job in the last day or two.

Perhaps it was my threats of not passing her probation that did it.

Well, whatever it was, I'm glad she's getting stuck in now.

The plans for the festival actually sound great. She's marked out a couple of the surrounding fields for the camping area and allocated the gardens nearest the house for where marquee tents are being erected to hold a variety of pretty out-there-sounding workshops.

They're having wood-fired hot tubs too, which have already arrived and are currently being set up round the side of the house where we get the most light.

The crew and organisers will be staying in the hotels' rooms and they'll be using the ballroom-cum-conference room for a mixture of yoga studio space and a dancefloor in the evenings. They've even got their own caterers, who will be taking over the kitchens, to provide a totally vegan menu for the duration of the festival, and they'll be using the dining room to seat people for meals. It'll be a bit of a squash, but she reassures me that no-one will mind this. Apparently, it's a very laid-back, friendly event.

The library will be doubling as an informal chill-out room where people can sit and read, or chat, as well as a space for musicians to perform. They're also planning on hosting a cabaret in there on the Friday night. Evidently, festival-goers volunteer acts to perform at it. It sounds like most people aren't professional artists or musicians, but it's open for anyone to showcase their skills or party tricks.

So that should be interesting.

Saturday night is party night with a dress-up theme and they'll have a series of DJs in the ballroom.

I have to admit, I'm actually intrigued to see how this goes. It's been a long time since this house has seen a proper party and it's making me feel nostalgic for my hedonistic uni holidays when my mates and I would take the place over for a week at a time.

It'll be great to see the place really come alive again.

Not that I'll be getting involved with the festival. I'm going to continue to keep a low profile, as I have done since moving here and opening the hotel. I wanted my fresh start to be about the house and the quality of the experience, rather than about me. Or my old man.

This really frustrated Tessa, who was all for using my fame to get punters in. But the last thing I wanted at that point was people coming to stare at me and ask awkward questions.

I'm so done with the whole fame thing.

So I definitely don't want people recognising me and another bloody meme making its way onto the internet.

Just as I'm trying to push the horror of this thought to the back of my brain, Dee comes striding into the hotel reception, where I've been checking on upcoming room bookings for the next couple of months – which are looking a little anaemic – and comes to a halt in front of me. Her cheeks are flushed and her eyes alive with what looks like excitement.

Wow. She really is a very attractive woman.

Another thought I have to push away.

Her sweet scent hits my nose and I breathe it into my lungs, feeling my body respond in a way that it hasn't before.

'Are you wearing a new perfume?'

She looks startled by my barked question.

'Er... um... yes! I bought it the other day. Don't you like it?'

'No, no, it's fine.'

It's more than fine. It's actually making me hard. I shift on the spot and link my fingers in front of me so my hands are shielding my groin.

'Okay, good. Mr Jacobson—' she begins.

'If you're not using "boss" any more, call me Jonah, will you. I can't be doing with all this *Mr* bullshit.'

She blinks at me, a little surprised by my cross interjection, then nods.

'Okay. Jonah. I need to allocate a room for the wellbeing volunteers to work from. Can I use the one next to your office? It would be the best place for it, I think, since it's out of the way and therefore quieter.'

'Sorry, the what?'

'Wellbeing team. They have people on hand who work as friendly contacts for the festival-goers. In case someone's having a tough time and needs someone to talk to. It's a really important part of the festival. It means everyone feels safe and heard if they have any issues with other attendees, or if they're struggling with their mental health, for whatever reason. There's a strong emphasis on consent at the festival – they even have dedicated workshops about it, which everyone's encouraged to attend – to really hammer home the civic-welfare ethos.'

I stare at her for a moment, processing all this. It actually sounds like a brilliant idea.

'And are these wellbeing people trained?'

'Yes. They're all professional therapists. They get free entry to the festival so they can enjoy the rest of it as a punter when they're not doing their shift. It's a system that works really well apparently.'

'Right. Okay. Well then yes, of course. They're welcome to use the room next to mine.'

'Thanks,' she says, giving me a broad smile. 'I'll get the staff to make it useable for that purpose. Maybe put some more comfortable chairs in there, if that's okay?'

'Sure.' I'm very much liking this new version of Dee. I hope she stays after the festival is over.

'Oh, and Jay, the guy organising the festival, says he's a fan of your music and he asked me to tell you that you'd be more than welcome to perform at the cabaret if you'd like to. There's no pressure, but it's an open, inclusive event, so everyone's welcome. The whole idea of the festival is that it's community led, so you're encouraged to participate in your own individual way.'

I hold up a hand, alarm making my shoulders twang with tension. 'Whoa there. I'm not intending to get involved with the event, just be discreetly on hand to protect the interest of the property and the business.'

I think I see a flash of disappointment in her eyes. 'Okay, no problem,' she says, with what sounds like forced conviction.

'I don't perform to the public any more,' I tell her, feeling a bit churlish now about refusing to play. But I made the decision for a good reason and I'm intending to stick to it.

'That's a shame, but I totally understand,' she says with a kindly smile.

I open my mouth to defend myself, then close it again. I don't owe anyone an explanation about why I decided to stop being a musician.

'Anything else?' I ask instead.

She blinks at my abruptness. 'No. That's everything. Thanks.'

Once again, I feel like a dick for being so short with her. But it seems it's best to be completely straightforward with Dee, so there's no room for misinterpretation.

Like that misunderstanding about the kiss she thought I might be interested in the other day. Admittedly, I'd been in an anarchic mood after seeing something online about Tessa and her new partner and so had been more receptive to Dee's flirting than usual. Perhaps I'd even flirted back a bit. It had felt good to feel wanted. But as soon as she made her move, I knew it was a bad idea.

It was the right decision to reject her advances. I'm sure of that now.

Pretty sure.

7

BEATRICE

Wandering around the beautiful grounds of the hotel, checking that we've got everything in place for the upcoming long weekend's event, I feel a swell of appreciation at the magnificence of the setting.

It's a real oasis of calm here.

Which is a balm after the tension of the last couple of days.

A change of venue at the last second has been an incredibly stressful thing to navigate, both for me and for Jay. He's had to make sure he's contacted everyone who bought a ticket and offer additional transport to anyone who's been put out from the change in location. Luckily, it seems that most people won't be affected, so it's not cost him much in monetary terms. But the mental load has been quite considerable. Hopefully, this means he'll be interested in holding the festival with us in the future again, as we'll be a known quantity from this point on.

Something Dee will have in her arsenal for when she comes back to take over.

I take a deep, calming breath, pushing away the strange new

tension that's invaded my chest at the thought of handing this back to my sister.

I should be pleased with what I've achieved in the last few days – and I am. But there's an unsettling feeling of having to let go of something I'm not quite prepared to give up yet.

The buzz I've felt from problem solving in the last couple of days is something I wasn't expecting.

And I'm loving working here at Gladbrooke House. It's such a beautiful place – something I'm going to really miss once I'm back in my basement office.

The setting here is something else.

The land surrounding the house is bordered by mature, ever-green trees on all sides, so any hint of the sights and sounds of the world outside are shielded from view.

Behind me, the Bath-stone-fronted house glows in the fading, late-winter sun and I realise I'm actually envious of Jonah for his family owning this magical place.

To the right of the house, the hot tubs, which are shielded by a dense hedge, are being heated ready for chilly guests to warm themselves through. Jay assures me that all the decorations that are being strung about the place are eco-friendly and made with repurposed materials. He has a team of artists and prop makers who take care of dressing the venues for the festivals and it's been a marvel to watch them transform the place into a winter wonderland.

To stretch my legs, I wander through a small thicket of trees a few hundred metres to the left of the house and find myself at a large lake. This is also surrounded by trees, making it completely private from the rest of the estate.

I sit on a fallen tree trunk and watch a group of ducks glide gracefully across the rippling surface. There's a sweet, musty smell in the air given off by a combination of the water and the floating lily pads and reeds dotted across the lake, which I breathe in deeply. I've always loved the scent of water, especially the mustiness of it. I can't quite explain why. It just does something provocative to my taste buds.

Relaxing back onto the rough bark of the log, I stare up at the sky and watch the birds wheeling above me, feeling for the first time in a long time a sense of being properly connected to the earth and nature. I've been working so hard in the last few years – all through my schooling, university degree, then straight into the business with Jem – that I've barely taken any time out to just be.

Completely forsaking the instruction of my own name. Bea. *Be.*

Huh. I'm not sure where that thought came from. I hope I've not been breathing in invisible floating spores from a patch of magic mushrooms nearby.

Ahh, but it's so wonderfully peaceful here.

I'm suddenly aware that I'm feeling something completely new.

I think it's contentment.

Now I know what I'm doing with this job, I'm loving being on my feet all day and outside in the fresh air for a lot of it. It's very different from my usual day-to-day experience of being tied to my desk in the office staring at words on a screen.

I remind myself, for the umpteenth time today, not to get too attached to this place, or this role. It's unlikely I'll ever be able to visit here again once I hand the reins back over to Dee. It might put her position in jeopardy again if Jonah even has an inkling that he's been duped by us.

I push away a shiver of disquiet. I'm doing this to help Dee out, I remind myself. And it's not like we're trying to trick something out of Jonah. He may be an arrogant, taciturn grump but I don't wish him any ill.

And I do feel bad about lying to him.

I'm distracted by the sound of my mobile ringing. Sitting up, I pull it out of my pocket and check the screen. My heart flips when I see that it's Dee calling me.

Uh oh, what now?

'Hi, Dee? Is everything okay?' I ask, the moment I connect the call.

'Hiya, Bea. Er, yes, all good here. How's everything going there?'

'Yeah, fine. Busy. Was there something you need?' I'm acutely aware of the impatience in my voice, but I don't have the brain space for chitchat with my sister right now.

'Er, no, not really. Just wanted to check in.'

'Oh. Okay. Well, everything's going to plan here. Don't worry.'

'As if I'd worry with you in charge,' she scoffs.

Is that a twang of bitterness I hear in her voice? Nah, she must just be fed up with sitting around in my flat. I hope she's not making a nuisance of herself and bothering Jem when he's trying to work.

'So, the funniest thing happened yesterday,' Dee says.

My stomach does a slow roll. Uh oh, this sounds like it has the potential to turn into something I'm not going to want to hear.

'Really? What?' I ask hesitantly, screwing up my face in readiness for the next disaster.

'Well, I was really bored and still in a lot of pain with my ankle, but I thought I might be able to help Jem out in the office with some basic things like looking at emails, you know?'

My heart sinks as I immediately start to worry about the new way Dee has found to annoy the crap out of my business partner.

'Dee, you need to leave Jem alone. You can't go distracting him. He's really busy at the moment, especially as I'm not there to take up the slack because I'm here doing your job for you,' I whisper into my phone, hoping to goodness that Jonah isn't about to burst out of the trees and confront me after overhearing my conversation.

I get up and look around me, but luckily the place seems deserted.

'Yes, I know that, Bea. That's why I was trying to help and not just sit around like a useless lump.'

I feel a surge of guilt at the hurt in her voice. 'Okay, sorry. So, what's the funny story?' I ask.

'It's just that I took some of those painkillers that Mum used to take for her bad back, so I could concentrate...'

Oh, no, this couldn't be good. Those were strong meds and ones Dee really shouldn't be messing with.

'And it was weird because they made me act a bit wild!' She giggles after saying this.

I can only imagine what that means.

'It was pretty funny though,' she adds when I don't immediately respond with a giggle of my own.

'Okay, well, for goodness' sake, don't take any more of them. You shouldn't use meds that aren't prescribed for you, especially when I'm not there to look after you.'

'All right, Bea, I know,' she says crossly. 'No need to mother me. I'm only telling you because it's a funny story. And anyway, I was fine in the end. Jem looked after me.'

My friend's face flashes into my mind and I can just picture the grim expression on his face, having to deal with a stoned – and what sounds like a potentially *frisky* – Dee.

Poor Jem.

I'm going to owe him big time for this.

'Anyway, then Dad turned up at your flat this morning. Just let himself in and strolled into the bedroom in his usual entitled way and he kind of got the wrong end of the stick about Jem being in bed with me.'

'What!' My exclamation is so loud, birds rise from the trees in alarm.

'Don't panic. Nothing happened. He stayed with me 'cos I got a bit anxious about being alone. Anyway, I didn't want to tell Dad that Jem was only looking after me because of the mistake with the meds, so he's now under the impression that we're a couple and that you're away in Scotland at a friend's mum's funeral rather than pretending to be me at my job at the hotel.'

'Oh my God, Dee.' I shake my head at the sky in utter bewilderment at my sister's innate ability to get herself into these ridiculous scrapes. Which she's now dragging me into too.

Before I can say anything else, Dee says, 'Dad actually came over to invite you and me on a business trip with him. Apparently, he's been trying to woo this hotshot billionaire so he'll invest in his business and sit on the executive board or something, which will be a major coup for Dad. The guy's a real family man, apparently, and makes a point of only working with people who have similar family values to him. As you can imagine, that's a bit of a stretch for Dad to prove. The man's not exactly father-of-the-year material.'

'That's a little unfair, Dee,' I say, though with less conviction than I'm sure my dad would want to hear. He's been good at paying for anything we need, but he's not exactly the touchy-feely type and the most attention we ever got from him when we were young was when he was giving us lectures about our future prospects. I know he loves us both, but he has a real problem showing it. His own dad was the same – emotionally restrained – or so our mum told us.

'Dad clearly thinks the guy needs persuading otherwise,' Dee continues, ignoring my interjection, 'so he wants us to go to this billionaire's swanky private Greek island, where we've been invited to join him for the weekend. Obviously, you can't go cos you're "in Scotland", so he's reluctantly suggested he and I go without you. He's promised me he'll pay off my student loan with some of the money he makes from this deal if I pretend to be a doting daughter while we're there. And,' she continues, before I can respond to this lunacy, 'because Jem's now my "boyfriend", he's asked him to come too, no doubt thinking Jem will keep me in line.'

'What!' I say again. 'Why can't this wait till I'm "back from Scotland"?'

'It's time sensitive apparently because the billionaire's off to some important summit, then climbing Everest or some such idiocy and Dad needs to lock in this deal before one of his business rivals gets in there first.'

'Right. I see.' I'm not sure how I feel about this, but it's not like I have the option to scupper it. I have to be here at the festival all weekend. I can't just walk away now and leave Jonah in the lurch. 'What about your ankle?'

'I've got some crutches and Jem will be able to help me if I need someone to lean on.'

I can't imagine Jem's wild about the idea of spending the weekend with Dee pretending to be her boyfriend and skivvy, but I imagine he thinks it's better to stay on my dad's good side. I wonder why he didn't put my dad straight about the misunderstanding though? He must have a good reason. I'll text him in a minute and check he's really okay with all this.

'I can't believe this is all happening right now. Talk about bad timing,' I grumble.

'I'm not exactly thrilled about it either, you know,' Dee says, tetchily. 'But this is the first time Dad's ever asked for my help and I want to show him I'm a worthy part of this family too.'

I sigh. 'Yeah, fair enough. But, please, Dee, you have to look after Jem while you're there. Be kind. And no monkey business, you get me?'

'I promise,' Dee says in her most solemn voice.

I'm not entirely sure whether to believe her, but I guess I really don't have a choice.

As soon as Dee cuts the call, I text Jem.

> Are you really okay to go on this trip with my dad and Dee? You can say no, you know. And what's this about you and Dee pretending to be a couple?!?!

His reply comes back a minute later.

> It's fine. I'm happy to help. I assume Dee told you what happened? She begged me not to tell him the truth and I felt sorry for her, so I agreed. I didn't think it would be a big deal to go along with it, then pretend we'd broken up the next time I saw him. What I didn't anticipate was your dad inviting us to go away for the weekend with him. I couldn't backtrack on it by then for fear of looking like an idiot. He's not a man I want to get on the wrong side of. Conversely, he IS someone I'd quite like to owe me a favour. Plus, I've never had the opportunity to visit a private Greek island. I'm planning on sizing up the area for when you and I make our millions and we've got some spare cash to splash around ;-)

I smile, relieved he doesn't seem too put out by all this nonsense and text back:

> Well thanks. You're a good friend and I
> appreciate you looking after Dee. I owe you big
> time for all this.

No sweat

I slide my phone back into my pocket, still not entirely convinced this weekend will go the way any of them anticipate.

But it's not my problem right now. The festival is. Speaking of which, I'd better get back there before Jonah finds me here and tears a strip off me for slacking off.

Ignoring a strange flip in my stomach at the thought of him, I stand up and take one long last look at the peaceful lake before making my way back towards the hotel.

* * *

Once back in the house, I wander into the kitchens to make sure everything's ready and available for the festival's catering crew.

Apparently, Pete's not going to be able to come this weekend and I've decided not to introduce his partner, Jay, to Jonah, so as not to make things awkward or complicated for anyone.

I didn't tell them that I'm posing as Dee this weekend because, firstly, I didn't want to ask anyone to lie for me and secondly, I was afraid Jay might reconsider holding the festival here if he thought there was anything screwy with the set-up. We need this to work in order for Dee to pass her probation and it's only a short amount of time I have to keep the ruse up. So, I've posed as Dee to do all the comms with Jay.

Thankfully, Jonah seems happy to let me just get on with the running of things.

In fact, he's been really chill about the whole thing up till now, which has surprised me. I thought he'd want to micromanage the hell out of it, but he seems reluctant to do anything client-facing. For someone as famous as Jonah is, I'm amazed he's not capitalising on it.

But then, from his grumpy manner, I get the feeling there's more going on under the surface than he's letting on.

There's a tale to be told.

Not that I should be interested in uncovering it.

I'm fully aware that I mustn't get emotionally involved with Jonah in any way.

Yet I can't help but be intrigued by him.

8

JONAH

By Thursday lunchtime, the house and grounds have been fully transformed into the latest venue to host the Terra Firmer Festival.

There's a real buzz about the place as the crew puts the finishing touches to the staging of it, as the first festival-goers begin to arrive and start setting up their tents and camper vans in the nearby fields. The crew have brought their own portacabin toilets and showers, so the house's facilities shouldn't get too much of a bashing. Dee tells me they're expecting about two hundred and fifty people to be coming and they have their own security on hand to make sure we don't get descended on by any gate-crashers. Not that that's ever been a problem before, she assures me.

I'm impressed with how the guy who runs the festival has been able to divert all his staff and volunteers to a new venue at such short notice. The fact we're only a few miles away from the venue he'd originally booked for it has benefited him and it seems his team, along with Dee, have been able to adapt the site plan to make it fit with our grounds and the layout of the house.

When I questioned whether people actually enjoyed going to a festival outside the summer months, she seemed to think it was actually a good idea. 'To ward off the winter blues.' Which makes some kind of sense, I suppose? I've definitely suffered with SAD before in the cold, mostly sunless months of an English winter, so I can see the logic behind it. We have to do something to naturally raise those depleted serotonin levels.

I have to admit, I'm a little nervous about how this weekend is going to go, though. But I can't worry about that now. It's a well-oiled train, fully in motion and there's no way to call a halt to it now that people have started arriving.

You know what? I've never seen so many people in leggings before in one place – both men and women. Most of the festival-goers I've seen arriving are wearing outfits in a kaleidoscope of colours, in every sort of fabric imaginable. There's an awful lot of fake fur, flowers and sequins on show. And the glitter – which I've been assured is strictly bio-degradable – is everywhere.

It's wild.

I'm already starting to regret my decision to stay hidden away. This long weekend looks like it's going to be a blast. There's a palpable feeling of excitement and purpose in the air and it's really brought it home to me how long it's been since I had any kind of fun.

I wander over to where the hot tubs have been set up and, from the sounds of it, are already thronged with people. I can definitely see the appeal of this feature in such cool weather. Even though it's been a fairly mild winter, there's still a nip in the air.

What I'm not prepared for, as I surreptitiously peek through the hedge that shields them from the house, is the nudity.

It's the most incredible thing. The people jumping in and out of the hot tubs seem not to be wearing a stitch and appear entirely comfortable with it.

In fact, no-one's batting an eyelid – except me. And that's only because I'm taken aback by the complete lack of self-consciousness in evidence.

It's actually really inspiring to see.

Freeing.

I'm half tempted to join in, but I know that would be a terrible idea. It only took one person to get out their phone and film the humiliating end to my relationship last year to make it the most watched meme on the internet for a while. Just when I was starting to slip out of the news cycle too. I thought moving here and maintaining a low profile would keep me out of the sight line of all those 'social commentators' who love to tear anyone with any kind of celebrity down.

Even though I'm not performing any more, the fact I'm my father's son means people are always interested in what I'm up to, even when it's totally banal and ordinary. I can't even go out for a meal without people staring and whispering about me, let alone get naked in a hot tub.

Just as I'm thinking this, I hear someone say loudly, 'So has anyone spotted Jonah yet? Do you think he'll grace us with his presence?'

'I can't imagine him just hanging out with the rest of us, can you?' a woman in the same hot tub says. 'Shame though. I'd love to chat to him about why he disappeared from the music scene. I always liked his band's music.'

Hearing this gives me an unexpectedly warm feeling in my chest. Until another voice pipes up and says, 'That dross? The guy's not a patch on his old man.'

The warmth disappears.

This is exactly why I made the decision to lay low in the first place. When you're as famous as I am, every fucker has an opinion on everything you do.

I slink off back to my office, cursing the accident of being born into the family I was once again.

* * *

I don't see Dee for a few hours as I determinedly stay at my desk, working through a backlog of emails, trying to push away my feelings of FOMO. When she talked me through what would be happening during the festival, she made it clear she'd be on site and on hand till late into the evening each night in case anything was required from the hotel, so I wouldn't need to get involved. But once again, I'm itching to see what's going on now. I can hear the happy hubbub of festivities floating in through my office window. There's live music being played somewhere in the house, a violin I think, and earlier I caught the sound of the piano coming from the library.

It made me yearn to go in there and sit and listen to it. Though I was also aware I was actually feeling the urge to go and get my guitar and play along. It's been a long time since I've experienced that. I've almost forgotten what it feels like to *want* to play music.

The judgement I've increasingly been subjected to about my musical talent has wrecked my enjoyment in performing though and I'm not exactly keen to invite it here in front of all these strangers.

As I'm finishing up for the day, ready to head next door to the small, one-bedroom ex-gamekeeper's cottage in the grounds that Tessa and I turned into our home while the hotel was being renovated, I decide to have one last walk around the site.

Not that I'm checking up on Dee. I think I can trust her to do a good job here.

But it's my hotel so I really should do a quick check-in, even if that means facing the stares and whispers of the festival attendees. It's ridiculous to think I have to hide away from all this in case I hear someone criticising me. I need to grow a thicker skin and this could be the perfect event to start doing that. The ethos of this festival is all about fostering a sense of community and kindness to every individual, no matter their background or circumstances, after all.

The hotel is thronged with cheerful, friendly looking people, who all seem to know each other. As I walk by them, I feel some of them turn to look at me, but there are no shouts or direct approaches and people let me pass by without bothering me, which I'm relieved about.

After checking upstairs, then walking into the kitchens, which are busy with caterers, then the ballroom and offices, finding everything is being looked after and is running as it should, I'm about to wander back out into the gardens, feeling a renewed sense of composure, when I hear the sound of a female voice singing a cover of a classic jazz and blues number accompanied by the piano, coming from deep within the house. I stop in my tracks to listen. It's beautiful. Heartfelt, haunting and full of emotion. So much so, it makes all the hairs on my arms stand up.

I walk towards the library, intending just to poke my head in and check it out for a moment before I head off home, but I'm completely floored when I see that it's Dee standing next to the piano, with the soft light from the low, end-of-the-day sun pouring in through the large picture windows, highlighting her silhouette and making her golden hair shine.

She looks like an angel.

The small audience in the library is as rapt by her singing as I am and I stand rooted to the spot, mesmerised by the beauty of her voice.

I can't tear my eyes away from her.

There's something so evocative in the musicality of her voice. As if she's actually feeling all the emotions she's singing about. It makes me want to know where that's coming from. What's happened to her to make her feel those things.

The song comes to a close and she smiles coyly as the whole room erupts into applause and whistles of appreciation. Turning to gesture towards the piano player that accompanied her, she claps her hands in gratitude and the whole crowd copies her, adding in more whistles.

The atmosphere in the room is electric. And uplifting. My skin rushes with a kind of excitement I've not felt in ages and the FOMO intensifies.

The piano player holds open his arms and Dee steps into them, bending down to receive a hug and a kiss on the cheek.

Even though it's probably only meant in a friendly way, an unexpected arrow of envy shoots through me, so that when she pulls away from the embrace and turns to see me lurking at the back of the room, I realise with a shot of regret that I have a scowl on my face.

Her warm smile is replaced with a frown of her own and worry flashes across her features.

I try to clear my expression as she makes her way towards me through the crowd of people, who are now chatting among themselves whilst the pianist noodles around with some background music.

'Jonah, hey,' she says as she makes it to where I'm standing by the door. 'Sorry. I promise you, I'm keeping an eye on things. Jay asked me to fill in for someone who was supposed to sing now.

Apparently, my friend, Pete – who I lived with during our second year at uni – told him I loved singing after the pub when we were all drunk and he wouldn't take no for an answer.' The stricken look on her face makes me realise she thinks I'm mad at her for showcasing her amazing voice, which couldn't be further from the truth.

'No need to apologise,' I tell her. 'I was just surprised to discover you're such a talented singer.'

Colour rises in her cheeks. 'Hardly talented.'

'Your voice is beautiful,' I reassure her.

She doesn't seem to be able to meet my eyes now, clearly finding it difficult to accept the compliment. Again, I'm a bit baffled by this. I would have expected her to react very differently, based on what I know of her. She's never struck me as the modest type.

The sofa facing the fireplace becomes free as a couple stand up to leave and I gesture towards it. 'Take a break for a minute?' I suggest.

She nods, if a little hesitantly, and sits down with me, our thighs close but not touching. The sofa is an old one and sags a little in the middle so we naturally lean in towards each other. I feel the heat from her body radiating towards me and breathe in her sweet scent, shifting uncomfortably as my body responds to it in a wholly inappropriate way again.

What the hell's got into me?

'Thanks,' she says, after a moment of awkward silence as we both shuffle around and finally settle ourselves into a more professionally suitable position. 'I've always loved singing. I used to be in the choir at school but I had to give it up because rehearsals were taking too much out of my study time.'

'Really? I'd have thought it was a good way to unwind.'

'I was too much of a swot for that.'

I frown, not entirely able to picture it. 'Apparently, music's brilliant for cognitive development though.'

She laughs, as if I've said something funny. 'Try telling that to my dad.'

I raise my eyebrows. 'He's not a fan of the arts?'

'You could say that.' Her frown returns and I have a strong desire to smooth it away with my fingertips. But I resist the impulse.

'He's never been that keen on us spending time on the arts. He's business-focused through and through.'

'Us?' I ask. 'You have siblings?' I suddenly find I want to know more about her. That the vulnerability I witnessed when she was singing has me by the throat.

She stiffens, as if I've asked too personal a question and I'm about to tell her she doesn't need to answer when she says, 'Yes. A sister.'

When she looks at me, there's a strange expression in her eyes. Perhaps she's a little wary now after I told her off for flirting with me the other day. I'm going to have to tread carefully here so as not to cross the professional line I drew. But a few questions about her background shouldn't be a problem.

'Do the two of you not get on?' I guess.

'No, no, we do. We're very different people, but I love her to bits. She can be a bit frustrating, but then can't all siblings?' She attempts a smile now and I nod back.

'Yeah, my brother used to drive me nuts when we were younger. See this scar?' I point to a small, white line above my right eyebrow.

She leans forward a little and peers at the place I'm pointing to. 'Yeah, I think so.'

'I got this when he pushed me into that fireplace.' I point at the offending structure: a large, carved Bath-stone fire surround and mantelpiece which is a beautiful feature of the room. 'It was after I beat him at Monopoly. I was fifteen and he was thirteen. I have to admit, I was gloating about it to piss him off, but even so.' I fake a look of abject hurt and I'm pleased to see her properly smile now.

'I didn't realise your family has had this house for so long.'

'Yeah, my dad bought it when I was a young kid and we used to spend some of our summers here. That's why I'm so keen to keep it in the family. Good memories. It has to pay for itself though; upkeep is not cheap and I'm determined to pay my own way.'

'So being a musician didn't make you rich then?' she asks.

A common misconception.

'Ha! No. Sadly not. When you're as famous as my dad, then yes, it does. But not a small fry like me. I never made it to the "big time", despite all the effort I put in.' I shrug, attempting nonchalance. I don't want her to know how much that failure has played into where I am with my life now. If I'd still been a musician, I'm pretty damn sure Tessa would still be around. She loved the fame, even if it was only the adjacent fame that came with being part of the music scene.

'So you don't play at all now?' I'm surprised to see she looks concerned by this.

I shrug. 'I love playing my guitar, but I'm done with performing for strangers. It's way too stressful. Especially when you have a powerhouse of a father like mine to live up to, but only a small percentage of his talent – or so the music press like to suggest.'

She frowns again, but this time in sympathy. 'That sucks.'

'Yeah. Big time. I've had this weight of expectation pressing down on me all my life. I kind of leaned into it and went a bit wild – got myself a reputation for partying a bit too hard, to be honest. People anticipated I'd follow in my dad's footsteps by being a musician too, but as soon as I took that path, they did everything they could to cut me down. I've had a lot of hate on social media from random strangers who seem to have taken real offence to me just being alive. People despise me for being a "nepo baby" even though I worked my arse off to get where I did. I used to love playing music, but I've always known I'll never be as good at it as my dad, so it got to the stage where I just thought, what's the point? So I stopped trying.'

'I'm sorry you were made to feel like that.'

'Yeah, well, it is what it is. Tessa, my ex, tried to push me to stay in the profession – it's what first attracted her to me I think; she's always been a music groupie – but it got to the point where it was making me miserable, so I quit. I was in a bad place for a while after that, so I wasn't a lot of fun to be around. It was one of the things – probably the main thing – that made her leave me. I wasn't so interesting when I wasn't a musician any more, just a depressed hotelier.'

She's looking at me intently and I'm suddenly aware that I'm in "too much information" territory.

'So tell me more about your sister. What does she do for a living?' I ask, to change the subject.

She starts and her expression suddenly becomes wary again.

Ah hell, I'm making a real fucking mess of this conversation. My professionalism seems to have gone out of the window since I saw her sing.

But before I can retract the question and suggest we both get back to work, she says, 'She's started a company with her best friend. They're making business software.'

'Oh. Right. That sounds, er, profitable.' I know fuck all about business software but I'm guessing anything in computing can bring in a good wage.

'It could be, if they manage to get the VC funding for it so it can get off the ground. It's tough going because there's a lot less money floating around for tech startups now, but they're both dedicated to making it work.'

'Right. Sounds stressful.'

She nods. 'It is. But she's pretty determined to make it succeed.'

'So determination runs in the family then?' I say with one eyebrow raised.

But she doesn't smile at that. 'When you have a father like ours, you don't really have a choice.'

'You don't get on with him?'

'Um. I do. Sometimes. But he's tough to please. Bea's always found it easier to get on with him. She's very focused, resilient and hard-working.'

'She sounds like a laugh a minute,' I say, laying on the irony.

But instead of smiling, she just blinks at me like I've personally insulted her.

'She just wants to be successful.' The sting of reproach in her voice makes me realise I've stepped over an invisible sibling-loyalty line. I admire her allegiance to her sister though. They're lucky to be that close. I barely ever speak to my brother now. We don't have a lot in common – never have.

It must occur to her that she's being a bit snippy with her boss because she clears her throat, gives me a perfunctory smile, and goes to stand up. 'I'd better get on with my job,' she says.

'Er, okay. Sure,' I say, giving her a nod when she turns back to look at me, perhaps checking that everything is still okay between us.

I watch her walk stiffly away, out of the library door, my heart sinking. I was actually having a good time, sitting and chatting with her. Getting to know her a bit better. I find I want to do it some more. Now we're getting into a better rhythm of working together, it's becoming increasingly easier to talk to her, which is a relief after our rocky start. I'm actually kind of surprised how much more I'm connecting with her now. There's something about her that invites confidences: an emotional intelligence I've not given her credit for. But she also seems to be much more professionally reserved around me now, after that talking-to I gave her about her job being in jeopardy. I'm craving to see the flirty, jokey Dee that I met when she first came here again though.

Perhaps I've been a bit too tough on her.

I should probably try and lighten things up between us.

Standing up, I nod to a few people who turn to smile at me as I make my way out of the library. There's such a great, positive atmosphere here at the moment and I'm going to be sad to lose it when the festival wraps up.

I make my way back to my house and let myself in, feeling the quiet press in on me. It's so different here compared to the party-like atmosphere in the big house. My skin itches with the urge to go back and re-integrate myself into the throng of people.

I feel cut off here, adrift. Alone.

Looking around, I notice for the first time in a while how dusty and oppressive it is in here. I've not done a thing to it since Tessa left. Perhaps it's time for a lick of paint.

Flopping onto the leather sofa, I let out a sigh and stretch my arms above my head, feeling my muscles scream in protest at how stiff I am at the moment. I need to do something to release this stress and tension that's bubbling beneath my skin.

My gaze alights on my guitar that's been propped in the corner of the room for the last year, taunting me. I've not been able to either put it away, or play it up till now. But suddenly, my fingers are itching to touch the strings again.

Levering myself up from the sofa, I go and grab it, sitting down to wipe off a thin layer of dust with the bottom of my shirt. The wood gleams softly in the fading light from the window.

It's such a beautiful instrument and it's a travesty for it to be sitting, unloved, in my living room. I can almost feel it crying out to be strummed.

So, for the first time in a year, I prop it on my thigh, hug it close to my body for a moment, then take a breath and begin to play.

9

BEATRICE

The next day, I'm kept incredibly busy going from marquee to marquee outside and room to room in the house, satisfying both the crew's and the attendees myriad – and amusingly eclectic – demands and requests. Someone needs a USB cable, someone else wants me to refrigerate some meds, another has lost a nipple ring, and I dash about like a woman possessed, sourcing and fixing and placating. But I love it. I feel useful and in control. I think I was born to do this job. I love the bustle and the challenge of it. And being away from the computer screen, which I'm normally chained to, is wonderful.

I keep catching glimpses of Jonah as I'm rushing from task to task, but he keeps his distance, seemingly giving me the space to do my job without interfering. Trouble is, every time I catch sight of him, my head goes a bit fuzzy and I forget what it is I'm meant to be doing for a moment.

Chatting to him in the library last night after he caught me singing was both wonderful – because of his compliments – and fraught with stress, as I tried to navigate his questions about me – or rather Dee and her sister – without tripping myself up and giving anything incongruous away to him. I was desperate to ask him to tell me more about himself, especially his last relationship, but I was worried that I wouldn't be able to remember it all and then not be able to recount it to Dee in enough detail.

The heat of his body in such close proximity to mine made me feel trippy and I'd had the weirdest urge to lean in closer to him. To feel what it would be like to touch him.

Sex appeal seemed to roll off him in waves and I was acutely aware of how attractive I found him, despite his gruff, grumpy persona.

I've never had a physical response to a man like that before – not with my first boyfriend during sixth form or for the couple of guys I slept with during my university days. Not even with the guy I had a short but intense holiday fling with just after I graduated.

But I also knew I had to keep my distance.

For the sake of my sanity. And for Dee's career.

Mid-afternoon, Jonah disappears and I breathe a sigh of relief that he finally seems content that things are going well here and he doesn't need to keep popping in to check on the place.

His mere presence, even in the periphery of my vision, has been making my nerves hum with awareness.

By nine thirty in the evening, I've finally managed to grab a bite to eat and I'm heading back over to the library to catch the end of the cabaret before I rush back to Dee's flat for a few hours' sleep, to recharge, ready for it all starting again in the morning.

The room is packed with people draped across all the armchairs and sofas in there, with everyone else crammed together on the floor, like a school assembly. There's a great atmosphere amongst the audience though, who are clearly enjoying the performances being showcased for their pleasure and there are whoops and calls of encouragement as the next act is called to the stage.

I manage to sidle my way into the room and squeeze into a tiny space next to the bookcase, gazing around me at the crowd of jazzily dressed festival-goers, who all look as if they come from another world. Another planet.

And there's Jonah again. He must have followed me in and is leaning nonchalantly against the wall near the door, watching the proceedings with such intense concentration, I wish I could see inside his mind. What must he think of all this? It's clearly more than he was anticipating, but so far he seems pretty cool with it.

It's a bit concerning that he keeps turning up wherever I am though.

Just as I'm thinking this, he turns and catches my eye, raising his eyebrows and motioning with a jerk of his head for me to join him where he's standing.

Warmth pools between my legs at the intense look in his eye. This is ridiculous. I really need to pull myself together. I absolutely cannot develop a crush on Dee's boss.

No matter how sexy he is.

Knowing I don't have a choice but to join him, I reluctantly leave my space by the bookcase and plot the easiest route through the crowd, which involves walking all the way around the edge of the room.

'Everything okay?' I ask once I've finally managed to pick my way through the crowd of people sitting between me and him.

'Yeah, good. I've changed my mind about playing in the cabaret.' He motions to a guitar I'd not noticed before, which is propped against the wall next to him. 'I figured, if you're brave enough to get up and perform in front of a bunch of strangers, then I should be too. And they seem like a friendly crowd.'

'Oh! Right. Well, great. I'm sure it'll be fine to add you to the running list,' I say, a little surprised at his change of heart, especially as he seemed so against the idea when I mentioned it to him before. I'm gratified by the notion that my own performance has inspired him to get involved too.

'And I want you to sing with me,' he adds, with a twinkle in his eye.

My heart flips over.

'Really?'

'Yes.'

'Oh.'

I'm flattered, of course, but also incredibly nervous about this request. It feels way too intimate a thing to do with him. But I can't say no, not when he's looking at me with such hopeful expectation.

Heat coils in my pelvis again as I stare into his eyes.

'W-which song are you thinking about performing?' I stutter, suddenly acutely aware of every nerve in my body standing to attention in the face of his intense charisma.

'How about "Why Try to Change Me Now"? Do you know it? Fiona Apple did an amazing cover and your singing yesterday reminded me of her, so I think it'd suit your voice perfectly.'

'I love that song. Yes, okay, I guess so.' My nerves are humming hard now, but not because I'm feeling shy about standing up and singing. I've seen how friendly and encouraging this crowd is, so I have no qualms there.

It's doing it with Jonah that's the major problem. It feels like we'd be crossing a line, somehow. Which is ridiculous of course and I'm probably reading way more into his invitation to join him than I should.

It's great that he wants to get involved with the community

spirit of it though. That's what these festivals are all about, after all.

And honestly, I'm once again warmed by his insinuation that he, a former professional musician, thinks I'm good enough of a singer to be happy to play music with me.

So after squeezing through the crowd to the person organising the event and asking if we could be added to the list – and getting an enthusiastic *yes* – I wind my way back and wait with Jonah for our turn, leaning against the wall next to him, barely aware of the acts being performed on the makeshift stage in front of us as I try hard to ignore his distracting presence next to me.

But it's impossible. Jonah Jacobson is not a man you can ignore, especially when he smells as good as he does.

I'm aware of people in the crowd turning to glance over in our direction too and I could swear that the atmosphere in the room has changed. It's now one of excited expectation.

My stomach swoops at the fear that I'll somehow let him down. I don't want his first foray back into performing to be wrecked by my nerves.

I mentally pull myself together. I'll just have to do the best I can. Hopefully, everyone will be too busy watching him to notice my performance anyway.

Finally, it's our turn.

We make our way over to the stage, nodding in appreciation of the loud applause we're given when we're announced as the next act. Jonah sits on a chair on the left, while I take up a position front and centre.

Luckily, I have a pretty good memory for song lyrics and the one he's suggested is one I've listened to a lot. Even so, I've got the words up on my mobile screen as a prompt, just in case. I clutch it in my sweaty hand as I step up to the mic and wait for Jonah to start playing.

As the beautiful sound of the first chords wash over me, all the hairs on the back of my neck stand up in appreciation.

Trying not to catch anyone in audience's eye, I start to sing and the whole room stills, everyone in it seeming to be listening intently to our performance. About half way in, I finally start to relax and enjoy myself, closing my eyes and losing myself in the joy of singing. It's been a long time since I've enjoyed performing. It was only ever a hobby when I did it at school, but I always loved the adrenaline rush I got from it.

I've not felt that in such a long time.

When did my life become so sedate?

Being here, in the hotel and at this festival, is really bringing it home to me how small and narrow-focused my world has become after leaving university.

I push the errant thought to the back of my mind and finish the song, the melodic sound of Jonah's guitar playing us out to silence. He really is a talented musician, his playing so confident and full of feeling. It's an absolute travesty that he gave up his career because of not feeling like he'll ever match up to his dad's talent.

It's not quiet for long after we finish the song. The roar of appreciation that builds, a few seconds after his last note fades away, is loud and enthusiastic. I turn to look at Jonah, but he's frowning down at the floor, seemingly deep in contemplation.

After taking an awkward bow, I step off the stage, intensely aware of him following me as I make my way through the jubilant crowd, who Jonah acknowledges with a raised, appreciative hand, and out into the relative cool of the hallway.

My mouth is dry from singing, so I make straight for the kitchen and head into the deserted butler's pantry to pour myself a glass of water from the large Belfast sink.

Jonah has followed me in and does the same, leaning back

against the counter to drink it. After draining my own glass and putting it carefully down in the sink, my hands trembling a little, I finally turn to look at him, wondering what sort of expression I'm going to see on his face.

He looks back at me steadily, his gaze intent on mine. That weird connection is there again, pulsing in the air between us.

My heart thumps hard against my chest.

'Thanks for doing that with me. I think we were a hit,' he says, breaking the tension by turning to put his own glass next to mine. 'It was fun performing with you,' he says, not looking at me now.

Heat rushes to my cheeks at his compliment. 'Good. For me too. I was pretty nervous in case I made you look bad.'

When he looks back at me, to my surprise, the corner of his mouth lifts in a grin, amusement dancing in his eyes.

My stomach does a strange, slow flip at the sight of it.

I think that's the first time I've seen him smile.

'Impossible,' he says, with real warmth in his voice.

And I love the way it makes me feel.

My entire body is rushing with a prickly, excited heat now.

Oh, my goodness, I'm deep in the danger zone here.

I'm aware of my heart beginning to race as adrenaline and need surge through me.

What have I got myself into? This is such a fine line I'm treading. I know I need to be a little bit flirtatious with Jonah – to act more like Dee – but not be *too* flirtatious so I don't move things on past where he and Dee were before her accident.

I absolutely can't allow anything to develop between us. I mustn't. It would put everyone in a really difficult position.

But perhaps I'm getting beyond myself here. So far, he's been nothing but professional towards me.

Apart from mentioning an attempted kiss by Dee that one time.

I wish she'd warned me that she'd tried it on with him. But then I know why she didn't: she was embarrassed about Jonah rejecting her advances. That doesn't tend to happen to her.

Perhaps it had something to do with him not being over his ex-girlfriend. There's always been a brittleness about him that speaks to him being in emotional pain. It makes my heart ache for him.

I realise I desperately want to make him smile at me again.

I've started to feel very differently about him, now I understand the extraordinary pressure of public interest, expectation and criticism he's had to live with all his life, thanks to his dad's success.

That would make anyone grumpy.

I lean my hip against the worktop and he mirrors me by doing the same, his gaze not leaving mine.

He opens his mouth, as if to speak, then shuts it again, a small frown crossing his face.

I can't tear my eyes away from him. He's so mesmerising to look at, with his dark, brooding gaze. So intensely sexy.

'What is it?' I ask, my voice shaky with nervous energy. I feel my heart pounding like mad in my chest now.

'I was just thinking...'

There's a long pause where he openly assesses me with his eyes and my entire body rushes with tingly heat again.

It's anticipation. Sweet, sexy anticipation.

'Yes?' I prompt softly, urging him to complete his sentence.

What's he going to tell me? Something good, I hope. Something positive.

'I—' He laughs softly to himself then shakes his head, his

gaze flicking away from mine, as if he's afraid his thoughts are too wild, too crazy.

'What?' I ask again, desperate to know what's going on in his head.

He snaps his gaze back to mine, as if making a decision. 'I was thinking how differently I'd react now if you tried to kiss me again.'

My heart seems to leap into my throat and I feel it pounding away there. Lust urges me forwards. To go for it. To do it. To see what would happen. But my brain tells me, *No, you mustn't. You can't.*

'Well, I probably shouldn't do that. *We* shouldn't do it. Since we're working together,' I whisper, having to force the words out of my mouth. It feels like the hardest sentence I've ever had to say in my life.

'No. You're right. We shouldn't,' he says, but there's no conviction in his tone. His pupils are dilated and his eyes are wide, still staring into mine, as if he can't look away.

It's mesmerising.

I can't look away either.

But I have to. I must. I can't let what I think is about to happen, happen. It wouldn't be fair on Jonah, not when he thinks I'm Dee.

I swallow hard and force myself to look away. Take a step backwards. Take a breath.

But he takes a step towards me, closing the distance between us again and when my deceitful body refuses to move away from him and our eyes lock, he takes another step forward. Then another.

We're so close now, I can feel the whisper of his breath on my lips. He's staring at my mouth, the way he did the first day we met. My skin tingles all over as we stand there together, trapped in the heat of mutual longing. My heart is thumping so hard, I feel like it must be shaking my whole body with the force of it.

Oh.

His hands move to cup my hips and I draw in a needy-sounding breath at the possessiveness of his touch.

This, it seems, is the sign he's been waiting for and before my brain can catch up, his mouth is on mine: hot and firm and purposeful.

Oh. My. God.

This feels so utterly right.

But it's so utterly wrong.

His mouth moves possessively against mine and I allow myself to sink into the kiss for the barest of moments, my whole body rushing with heat and a deep, heavy sense of hunger.

He understandably takes this as a positive sign and deepens the kiss, sliding his tongue against mine and drawing my hips even closer to him so I can feel the hardness of his erection against my belly. The awareness that he wants me this much sends a wave of pleasure through me, which pools between my legs, making me ache to be touched more intimately there.

I can tell by the way our bodies are responding to each other that sex with Jonah would be spectacular.

Seeming to feel the same way, he lifts me up onto the counter, pressing himself between my thighs and I feel his hands move up to my breasts. He rubs his thumbs against my tight nipples, which strain against the thin material of my top and send tendrils of pleasure shooting through my entire body.

I wonder wildly for a second whether I could come from being touched like this. It certainly feels like a possibility right now.

But, deep in the sensible side of my brain, I know I have to stop this.

I have to.

But he tastes so good. So right.

Wake up to yourself, Bea!

I put the flats of my hands against his chest and with every ounce of willpower I possess, push against him, so he's forced to take a step backwards and break the kiss.

His pupils are blown as he looks at me in pained confusion. 'What is it? I thought you were as into this as I am. Did I read it wrong?'

'No. Yes! I... I'm not sure.' I can feel my cheeks burning with heat.

God, I need to pull myself together.

'What's going on, Dee?'

The sound of my sister's name brings me up short and cements my decision.

I have to stop this in its tracks *right now*.

I slide off the counter and take a deliberate step away from him, trying to school my errant body into calming down.

'The thing is... about that time I tried to kiss you,' I begin, thinking fast. 'I should explain about that. I'd, uh, twisted my ankle and was taking some strong painkillers, so I could still do my job, and they had a strange effect on me. They made me a bit, er, forward. So I really should apologise for my inappropriate behaviour while I was on them.'

'Painkillers?' He looks incredulous, and honestly, who can blame him. If it wasn't for Dee's story about her own experience the other day, I probably wouldn't buy it as an excuse either.

'Look, the thing is, I really want to be professional here,' I say, hating myself for the lie. And for the pained expression on his face that's entirely down to me. 'I think you're an amazing person, but I'm really serious about wanting to do a good job for you, so I don't think we should be more than colleagues. We should keep those lines clear. I'm really sorry if I gave you the impression I wanted more.'

He rubs a hand over his hair, then shakes his head, looking up at me from behind his dark brows.

It's the sexiest thing I've ever witnessed. And the saddest.

'Okay, I accept you don't want anything to happen here and that's obviously fine. I respect you and I'll keep my distance from now on.' He pauses and keeps looking at me with that dark, sexy stare. 'But I don't understand what's been going on here. I'm a bit lost, Dee.'

I swallow hard, feeling like a total bitch. I'm not surprised he's so confused about my actions when in his mind, a combination of me and Dee is actually one and the same person.

He must be starting to think I have a split personality.

Which, if I think about it, is actually bang on the money, in a way.

I'm discombobulated because this feels like it's moved very fast to me, but of course it won't feel like that to Jonah, because he's known Dee for a few weeks now, so in his mind, he's right in the middle of starting a potential relationship with her.

Ugh! What a mess.

I want to cry.

'I'm so sorry. I never meant to make this difficult for you,' I say, truthfully this time.

His frown stays in place while he studies me for a few moments longer, perhaps waiting to see whether I'll change my mind again. But when I don't say anything else and just stand there like a lemon, digging my nails into my palms, he finally gives me one last curt nod and leaves the pantry.

I watch him go, his broad shoulders tense and his head slightly dipped in what I assume is disappointment. Pushing away the surge of guilt I feel at being the harbinger of his gloom,

I remind myself that Dee can fix all this once she's back, if she wants to. He's clearly into her, so I'm sure she'll be able to make up a feasible excuse to get him back on side.

I try very hard not to allow a bitter swell of jealousy in my gut to rise any further.

He's never been mine to have. And I promised myself not to get involved in any distracting relationships for a while anyway.

Jonah Jacobson is not the guy for me and he never will be.

10

JONAH

Dammit! How the *hell* did I read that so wrong?

I pace about, back in the cottage, cursing my bad judgement – again!

Clearly, I was high on adrenaline after feeling so relieved and positive about our performance – probably because it was the first time I've enjoyed performing in a very long time – and I misread the signals.

I could have sworn she was into me though. Especially after she tried to kiss me the other day. But it turns out she was just high on prescription drugs.

Or so she says.

That has to be bullshit, doesn't it? It's certainly the most far-fetched excuse I've ever heard. But then it might account for the change in personality I've witnessed recently.

Mightn't it?

Flopping down onto the sofa, I put my head in my hands, my fingertips digging in to my forehead.

Argh! What's she playing at? Is there something going on here that I'm just not seeing? I know I'm being completely paranoid, but does Tessa have some hand in this? But why would she? She's not made contact with me at all since leaving and she has no skin in the game here financially. It was my money that paid for the place to be renovated and because we weren't married and don't have any kids, I don't owe her any maintenance. Not that she's ever asked for it.

So what's going on then? Is this some kind of twisted game that Dee's playing with me? First coming on to me hard, then backing off fast. Trying to get me hooked into something with her, something she can control? But why would she do that? It doesn't chime with anything I've seen of her in the last few days.

Shit! What's happening to me? Tessa did a real number on me when she ripped my trust to shreds and it seems to be having repercussions through my entire life. Am I destined to always read women and their intentions wrongly?

Jeez, I hope not.

But then maybe it's not such a bad thing for me to be on my guard now. At least I won't be taken for a fool again if I'm being vigilant for it.

Anyway, it seems clear I need to separate how I've started to feel about Dee recently from our working relationship. I don't want to mess things up and lose a really good employee when I've only just found her. And on the surface, she seems keen on keeping things professional between us too.

If only my body would get the memo. I'm still turned on from kissing her, then not being able to take things further. I haven't felt this level of need for sex in ages and now I'm supercharged with it.

I stand up and start to pace the room again, not sure what to do with myself. Only one thing for it: I need to take care of this incessant urge myself before I'll be able to sleep. With that thought in mind, I pop the button on my jeans, slide down my fly and take my cock in my hand, picturing what I would have done to her amazing body if she'd not called a halt to things. I relive the feeling of her full breasts under my hands and the way her hard nipples pressed urgently into my palms. So fucking hot. I imagine how wet she would be for me when I slid my fingers inside her, finding the exact spot to give attention to, turning her wild and pliant under my touch. I imagine the expression on her face when she climaxes, moaning my name. I come hard, revelling in the blissful release as my body finally gets the relief from the sexual tension I've been holding at bay for the last few days.

* * *

In the morning, I wake up with another iron-like erection, having dreamt about Dee and our near miss, which my addled subconscious turned into a very definite hot hit.

I try to shake off the craving to make it real that's got me by the throat as I scoff down some breakfast, feeling as though I've run a marathon already this morning.

Wandering over to the house, I find an early-morning yoga session in full flow on the front lawn. The attendees are contorting themselves into impossible-looking poses and letting out loud, visible breaths into the cool, morning air.

The sun has made another appearance today and it's making the dew on the grass glint and shimmer as far as the eye can see.

As I walk into the house, I hear the sound of dance music pounding away, coming from the direction of the ballroom. Poking my head around the door to it, I'm amazed to see a large crowd of people dressed in full-on dance gear throwing themselves around to the beat, as if they're all at a rave. I stand, dumbfounded, watching them, feeling a weird sense of displacement.

It's so strange to see people dancing like this in the bright, morning sunlight.

A guy in a furry, turquoise onesie squeezes past me into the room, giving me a grin and a nod of greeting.

'Hey,' I say to him. 'Has this been going all night?'

'No. It started at seven this morning. It's a great way to start the day. The best kind of exercise!' he says and dances away from me into the crowd, whooping and punching his fists into the air in time to the music.

I stay and watch the joyful revelry for a minute more, fighting another urge to join in with the fun. I really shouldn't allow myself to be enticed by it. I'm here in a professional capacity and I can't let myself get drawn into what's happening here. I have my reputation – what's left of it – to think of.

It occurs to me now that the festival has reminded me of how much I loved partying in my former life and that's probably had some bearing on the way I acted towards Dee last night. I'm suddenly angry with myself for letting my dick get in the way of common sense.

I'd decided not to get drawn into a fling with her but I'd gone and let myself be side-tracked by the idea of it anyway.

I sigh and turn away from the dancing.

Some days, being an adult isn't a lot of fun.

Outside, more people are milling around now, yawning and stretching in the soft, morning sunshine.

Feeling a sudden weariness descend on me, I turn back towards my cottage. I suspect I'm going to need strong coffee if I'm going to get through today.

Back in my kitchen, I make myself a double espresso and add two spoonsful of brown sugar to it before knocking it back. I wince a little as the hot liquid burns the back of my throat, but the warming sensation of it hitting my stomach gives my spirits a lift.

I should get back out into the sunshine and have a walk in the fresh air. Sitting inside my house and brooding all day about what happened last night would not be helpful.

So, I drag myself out again and take a walk over to the apple orchard, avoiding the lake – a place I've not been able to visit since the thing that happened there trashed my relationship and my reputation – and wander through the leafless trees with their twisted and gnarled branches standing stark against the grey-blue sky, drawing in deep lungsful of cold, fragrant air. It's so peaceful here, even with the low-level hubbub of the festival waking up humming in the distance.

I had such high hopes for this place when I first convinced my dad to let me take it over, but it all ground to a halt when Tessa left and I've not quite found the impetus to get things going again. I was hoping Dee might be the one to help lead that, and I guess she might still, based on the effort I've seen her put in in the last few days.

In fact, focusing on that would be a good way to get past the awkwardness that's bound to be there between us now. Feeling in a more positive mindset, I set off back to the festival to see if I can find her and clear the air quickly so we can move on from it.

Since I've been away from the site, the rest of the attendees seem to have emerged from their tents and are strolling towards the large marquees where the workshops are being held before lunch is served.

Outside each of the tents, there's a blackboard with the name and a short description of the event written in white chalk on it. I walk past each one, reading, with increasing interest, about what's about to take place inside.

There appears to be a 'Cuddle-in' in one of them.

Intrigued, I poke my head into the tent and see a large group of people sitting or lying around on a ground sheet covered with cushions and furry rugs, all hugging someone close to them. There's nothing sexual about it – everyone is fully clothed, but there's a lot of contented-sounding sighing going on.

My skin tingles at the thought of being held like that again. It's been a long time since I cuddled anyone and after the aborted kiss with Dee last night, my body is back on high alert for physical contact.

Just as I'm about to step out of the tent again, the workshop leader calls out in a soothing voice for everyone to swap partners. There's a big shift in movement as everyone untangles themselves from their cuddling partner and moves to wrap themselves around someone new, first asking that person's permission. It seems, from the way they're being so polite, that they don't all know each other. It blows my mind for a second to see everyone so open to being that physically close to a stranger. It's actually really cool though. If only this was a more common practice in the 'real world', there might be a lot less loneliness.

With that thought swirling through my head, I back away quietly and stroll over to the next tent, wondering what I'll find happening in there.

It's a shibari workshop.

People are sitting in a large circle, each with a partner, and with lengths of rope laid out neatly on the floor in front of them. The instructor is demonstrating on a volunteer how to safely tie someone up. They've already had their legs tied and are now having their torso bound in an intricate pattern of rope and knots, which looks a bit like a corset. It's actually quite beautiful and I'm mesmerised by the skill of the person doing the tying.

Again, I back out quietly, feeling like a bit of a peeping Tom.

In the next tent, everyone is lying down on the ground while a couple of people walk slowly between them, playing percussion instruments like bells and gongs in overlapping, soothing-sounding waves. According to the blackboard, this is a sound bath. I've heard about these, how they can be good for stress, but I've never tried it myself. I'm not sure I could allow myself to sink into it enough to let it do me any good though. I'm definitely too strung out at the moment to lie still for long enough for it to have any impact on my rattled inner calm anyway.

I'd hoped, after moving here from the noise and chaos of London, that I'd finally start to find the peace that's always eluded me – except when I'd been staying here at this house. But the stress only seemed to increase as I came to realise that Tessa wasn't happy here.

A familiar sadness settles over me as I remember the good times we'd had together, mostly in my hedonistic, partying days.

I genuinely loved her and thought I was going to spend the rest of my life with her. She was my ideal woman: smart, funny, charismatic and an incredibly fun person to be around. It always felt like an adventure, being with her.

But I guess I wasn't enough for her. It seems it was my fame, or rather my dad's fame, that drew her to me and kept her around, but as soon as it was just me and her, it became clear I wasn't enough on my own. She needed more than I could ever give her.

And she definitely didn't need quiet like I did.

In fact, I think she actually thrives on chaos and busyness and noise.

Coming out of the tent, I'm aware of that sense of restlessness from this morning has returned. It's like there's something else I should be doing, but I'm not sure what that is.

Then I spot a familiar figure in the distance, going into one of the other marquee tents and something in my brain clicks into place. I've been hoping to see Dee, to smooth things over, and here's my opportunity. Perhaps if we talk and maybe get to laugh about what happened, it'll be okay. We'll be able to get past it and my sense of agitation will pass.

So, I stride after her and make it into the tent in time to see her being handed a hula hoop by a woman wearing an all-in-one sequined leotard and a headdress made of beads.

Dee has a quick word with her, then smiles and walks into the middle of the room where there's a space between people already attempting to get their own hoops to stay up on their waists by rocking their hips in a thrusting, sort of circular motion.

It takes me back to my infant school days where our teacher used to try, and mostly fail, to get us to be co-ordinated enough to do this in a PE lesson. I was always useless at it and ended up getting sent to sit on the side when I point blank refused to do it. So, when someone comes over and tries to hand me a hoop, I wave them away and move to the side to watch how Dee fares with hers.

It doesn't seem to take her long to get into the swing of it and as I lurk at the back watching her, I feel even more like a peeping Tom. There's something quite erotic about the sight and I'm unable to drag my gaze away from her. She's so graceful in the way she moves, as if her body is entirely fluid and one with the hoop. The small smile playing about her lips makes me wonder about what makes her tick in other situations: what makes her happy, excited, what turns her on...

I tug down the front of my shirt to hide the growing interest in my trousers. Dammit. I really need to stop thinking about her as a woman and concentrate on the fact she's my employee and very keen to keep that line drawn between us.

It's so hard to do that when she's moving the way she is. With such confidence and abandon.

But I have to, because that's what we agreed.

'Hey, Dee. Can I talk to you for a second?' I call over the music.

She doesn't look round, just keeps on hula hooping.

I'm pretty sure she would have heard that; it's not that loud in here.

'Dee?' I shout a little louder.

Still no reaction. That's weird. She's not ignoring me, is she?

'Delilah!' This time, my slightly aggravated shout gets her attention and she jumps and spins round to look in my direction, looking first a little shocked, then wary.

'Can we have a quick chat?' I call, in a less aggressive tone this time.

She frowns, as if she's working out whether she really wants to join me right now. Then her expression clears and she gives me an awkward-looking wave. 'Um. Yes, sure. Okay,' she calls back.

Her uncertainty gives me pause. Is she worried about being around me now?

After letting the hoop drop to the floor, then stepping out of it and handing it to one of the people running the workshop, she strides over to where I'm standing. Is it my imagination or is she nervous? Her hands flutter at her sides as she picks her way between the people between us, then smooth down her thighs as if she's trying to tidy the skinny jeans she's wearing.

My heart sinks at the realisation that she's probably going to be really uncomfortable around me now.

I silently curse my misunderstanding of the situation last night.

I still can't believe I got it so wrong.

It makes me question what else I've got wrong recently.

Unease settles on me like a heavy blanket.

'Let's go outside,' I suggest when she reaches me. I really don't want an audience for this conversation.

She nods and follows me out of the tent and onto the lawn. Most people seem to be either in a workshop or still asleep so there's no-one in our vicinity.

'Hey,' I say.

'Morning,' she says with a tight smile.

'Enjoying yourself?'

Her face falls and she clears her throat, looking castigated. 'I'm in the process of checking the workshop leaders have everything they need. I just stopped for a second to have a quick go with the hoop.'

I hold up a hand. 'I didn't mean to suggest you weren't doing your job properly.' Frustration rattles through me. Is this what it's going to be like from now on? Jesus, I hope not. 'Look, I know I've made things awkward between us after what happened last night. I just wanted to apologise for that. I read the situation all wrong, clearly.' I hear the gruffness in my voice and hope she doesn't think I'm angry about it.

I'm not. Just embarrassed. And a little bit fucking frustrated.

'No need to apologise. Seriously,' she says. And she sounds like she really means it too.

I relax a little.

There's an odd expression on her face that I've never seen before though and it stops me from feeling completely convinced that we're back to where we should be. I guess we need a bit more time to regain our equilibrium.

There's a muffled scream then a *whump whump* sound from the tent to the right of us and we both turn to look at each other with concern. That doesn't sound good.

As one, we turn and hurry towards the tent entrance. I push aside the canvas door and enter the tent in a rush, intent on finding out what the hell's going on in there, my heart thumping hard.

I come to an abrupt stop, with Dee nearly bumping into me, as I take in the sight of a large group of people, all armed with pillows. They're swinging away at each other with them, aiming for each other's torsos or legs, their faces showing a mixture of determination and elation. There are shouts and squeals of delight as they lay into each other, their soft weapons of choice making the gentle *whumping* sounds we heard from outside.

'Pillow fight!' Dee says on a gasp of relief and amusement.

'Here you go,' someone says to our right, tossing us both a pillow covered in a soft, cotton pillowcase. 'Get stuck in!'

I turn to look at Dee to see what her reaction is to this bizarre instruction.

She grins back at me and raises her eyebrows in question.

Am I up for it?

Yes. I think I am.

And I'm determined to get the first blow in.

Without a word, I raise one eyebrow in a show of challenge, then quickly swing the pillow forward in a gently swiping motion, connecting with her left arm.

Her eyes widen in mock outrage and she swings her own pillow in a wide arc, catching me on the hip.

There's a moment's pause, where we stare intently at each other, then, suddenly, with tacit understanding, we go at each other properly, landing blow after blow on each other's back, legs, shoulders. Shrieks and giggles escape from her as she takes a volley of soft thumps from my pillow, before retaliating with her own wide, on-point swing, that lands right in the middle of my back.

Even though it doesn't hurt a bit, I let out a sharp exhalation of breath as it's knocked from my lungs.

I turn to see her double over with laughter, her eyes sparkling and her cheeks flushed.

It hits me, like another blow to my body, just how beautiful she is.

This has the effect of suddenly sobering me up and I lower my pillow, raising a hand in defeat, fighting back the renewed rush of desire I've been shoving away hard since waking this morning.

Dammit.

'Okay, I concede. You win,' I tell her, not able to look her in the face now. If I do, I'm afraid I might do something stupid, like try to kiss her again.

There's a small pause, then out of the corner of my eye, I see her drop her own pillow onto the floor next to mine.

'Excellent,' she says, but I hear a hint of disappointment in her voice. It seems she was having fun, knocking seven bells out of me. 'I suppose I'd better get on with my job.'

I nod, still not meeting her eyes. 'Yeah, me too.'

We wave our thanks to the person leading the pillow-fighting orgy, leaving the rest of them still at it, and make our way back out of the tent.

'One last tent to check on here,' Dee says, heading towards the final one in the row. A thumping base begins from somewhere inside it. I glance at the blackboard next to the door and see that *Lube Wrestling* is written on it.

What the hell?

Intrigued and, if I'm honest, reluctant to walk away from Dee right away, I follow her, with some trepidation, into the tent.

There's a big group of people all crowded round a large child's paddling pool, its primary colours garish against the natural-coloured tones of the tent. In it are two people, one male, one female, both dressed in swimming costumes and nothing else apart from a single sock each. The pool appears to have about an inch of viscous-looking liquid in the bottom of it. From its thick, shiny consistency, I can tell it's not water. It's lube. And both people in the pool are covered in it. It shines on their skin, giving them the look of two seals fresh from the sea.

Except they're doing something I can't imagine seals ever doing.

They're wrestling, attempting to pull the lone sock off the other's foot, contorting themselves into impossible-looking shapes around each other's bodies and sliding around the pool in their attempt to evade the grasp of their opponent on their own sock.

It's the most ridiculous, hilarious thing I've ever seen.

The crowd are going wild for it, a chorus of cheers and hoots emanating from them as the music pounds away from a speaker nearby, driving the participants on.

'Fancy having a go at that next?' I jest, turning to quirk my eyebrow at Dee, then immediately worrying she might misconstrue that as a come on.

'That's a hard no from me.' Luckily, she seems to have taken it as the joke I meant it to be.

I grin, sweeping a hand over my hair, feeling my earlier jitters returning. Time to go.

'Okay, well, I'll see you later at the party.'

'Great,' she says. There's an awkward pause where she smooths her own hand over her hair, looking a little taken aback when her fingers reach the end of her bob, as if she wasn't expecting it to end there.

Apparently, she's still as nervous as I am about where our relationship currently resides.

'See you in a bit,' she mutters, before turning on her heel and striding away from me and out of the tent, her gait a little less graceful than usual on the uneven ground.

11

BEATRICE

After a day of workshops, hot-tubbing and yoga, the dress-up party begins with a bang at nine o'clock.

There are people everywhere. Some in full body paint – that's got to be chilly! – some in costumes in a medley of colours, fabrics and styles, but all – if only loosely – are following the theme of Northern Lights.

The vegan banquet was cleared away from the ballroom an hour ago and it's now set up as a dancefloor, ready for the evening's DJs' sets and the library has been allocated as the chill-out space and live music room again.

Outside, a large group of people are juggling with fire batons and flaming hoops to the rhythm of bongos, their movements deft and mesmerising, the flames carving sparkling trails through the dark night that's descended on us.

I stride around the site, checking the crew are all happy and have everything they need for the evening. I don't need to worry though; Jay is exceptionally organised and well-practised by now at running these events. I'm not surprised they're so popular. His summer event a couple of years ago was featured in a 'Best

Events of the Summer' article in one of the left-leaning papers which was amazing publicity and, according to Pete, gave his attendance numbers a real boost.

Music and a happy, low level of noise seems to emanate from every corner of the festival as crowds of partygoers move from event to event, talking animatedly. Everywhere I look, there is colour and movement. The place feels alive with joy and a celebration of life.

I actually feel a bit out of place in my smart work gear and wish I'd thought to bring a costume for myself so I'd blend in a bit better. I'm starting to yawn a lot now, after a bad night's sleep. I'd not been able to clear the memory of Jonah lifting me onto the counter and kissing me with such intent, my whole body raged with a need to feel him moving inside me. I kept reliving the way his mouth felt on mine. It was so assured. So right. The smell of him had intoxicated me, sending shivers of pure lust all through my body.

My exhausted brain had finally allowed me to drop into a troubled sleep in the early hours, only for me to then be woken again at six o'clock by my alarm, in order to give me time to get back to the hotel before the festival got going again.

So, I'm dying to take a few minutes to myself and perhaps chug a coffee to try and wake up a bit now.

It's going to be a long night, judging by the energy I'm seeing pulsing through the party.

After checking the ballroom and seeing the dancefloor is happily heaving, with people dancing wildly to an eighties pop track, I decide to retire to my office for a while to regroup.

Mercifully, the room is relatively quiet compared to the rest of the site and I sink into my chair, my ears ringing after being battered by the loud music, feeling relief at being able to sit down for a few minutes and gather my thoughts.

I've not seen anything of Jonah since this morning when we ended up having a playfight with those pillows, which was actually a cathartic release from the tension that still lingered between us after last night.

My phone buzzes in my pocket, startling me, and I pull it out and check who's calling, wondering whether Jonah's trying to find me. The inappropriate excitement I feel quickly fades when I see Dee's name on the screen.

Not that I'm unhappy to see it's her. I've been wondering how she's getting on, stuck on an island with our father.

I stand up and walk over to the window, steeling myself to hear all about it.

'Hey you, how's it going?' I say into the phone after pressing the green handset symbol.

'Not great,' my sister replies.

My mood sinks lower. Now what?

'What's up?' I ask, mentally preparing myself for another of Dee's crazy tales.

'The bloody weather's up, that's what!' Dee says, her breath expelling in a hard sigh, like she's been punched in the gut.

'The weather?'

'Haven't you seen the news? There's a bloody typhoon or something on the way. It's been raging away over on this side of the planet. Our island seems to be in the path of the epicentre so we're stuck here till it passes over. No planes or even boats out of here for a few days. It's too dangerous, apparently.'

From the tone of her voice, it sounds as if she'd rather risk a terrifying, wholly inadvisable journey than be stuck there with our dad.

'Right. Okay. Well, hopefully it won't be for long. Those things tend to blow over quickly, I think.'

'Not quickly enough,' Dee mutters.

'Is Jem okay?' I ask, even more worried for my business partner who's not only stuck with my father, but my grumpy sister too.

'He's fine,' Dee says stiffly.

'Well, don't worry about things here. We're okay. Just stay safe and get back as soon as you can.'

'I was thinking... perhaps you could pretend to twist your ankle before work on Monday morning, once the festival's finished. Then you can ask Jonah for a couple of days off to recover. I should be back by then and it won't look strange when I come back with a bit of a limp.'

My stomach does a weird flip at the thought of things coming to an end so abruptly here and handing this role back to Dee. I shake it off. It's her job and she's right; we need to be tactical about how to get her back here without things looking odd.

'Er, yeah. I guess so.'

'Great. And you're really okay holding the fort for the rest of the weekend?'

'Totally.'

Dee lets out another sigh. 'Thanks, Bea. Well, I'll see you soon, I hope. Assuming the island doesn't sink before we manage to make it off here.'

I smile to myself. My sister is such a drama queen.

'I'll see you soon,' I say. 'Don't do anything silly,' I add.

'What do you mean, "something silly"? I might make the odd mistake but I'm not wilfully negligent!' Dee sounds affronted.

'No. Sure. Sorry. I don't know why I said that. Just stay safe. And look after Jem, will you. It can't be easy for him being trapped there.'

'Hmm.'

Her lack of positive response gives me a moment of worry. But there's nothing I can do from here and to be fair, Jem's perfectly capable of looking after himself. I don't know why I'm worrying.

'I'd better go,' Dee says and before I can say anything else, she cuts the call.

I let out a loud sigh and slide my mobile back into my pocket. My sister is a walking disaster area. It's one thing after another with her, although to be fair, she doesn't have any control over the weather so I should probably give her some leeway with this one.

'Are you Dee?' someone asks behind me and I turn around to see a tall, slim man wearing a rainbow-print catsuit standing there with his right hand thrust towards me.

'Yes,' I say. 'How can I help you?'

'I cut myself when I put my hand into my washbag and caught my finger on my razor. It won't stop bleeding. I think I might need some butterfly plasters or something. Someone thought you might have a medical kit I could look in.'

Before I can stop myself, I glance down at his proffered hand and see the deep cut he's referring to at the end of this pointer finger, from which bright, glistening blood is escaping in pulses and running down his hand.

My stomach lurches and I experience the unwelcome sinking feeling of horror I get when I see an injury.

I suck in a deep breath.

I know I mustn't let it get to me – I'm supposed to be in charge and the go-to person for help – but my squeamish mind has other ideas. All the blood seems to drain from my head and it suddenly feels too heavy for my neck to hold up. A darkness is descending over my vision, as if someone's drawing a blind down over it and gravity appears to have increased tenfold and is pulling me down to the ground. My body is no longer able to fight against it and I give in to it, dropping to the floor in a crouch then pressing my forehead against the carpet, praying I won't pass out completely.

'Hey? Are you okay?' I hear the guy say, in a distant-sounding voice. It's as if all my senses have been dulled and the only thing I can hear properly is my blood rushing in my ears.

'I'm... I'm okay...' I whisper, but I sound completely unconvincing. 'Be okay in a minute...' I'm breathing in short gasps now, trying to get more reviving oxygen into my body.

'Dee?' I hear a deep, familiar-sounding voice say nearby. But whoever it is, it sounds like they're underwater.

My mind is in freefall. I can barely concentrate on anything except the feeling that I'm about to be sick.

'She's not here; she's stuck on an island,' I say, wishing my sister *was* actually here right now to look after me. She is always really good at pulling me out of these states. She has a knack of saying just the right thing to distract me.

I'm aware of someone kneeling down next to me and I feel the weight of a hand on my back. 'What's going on? Are you ill?'

I shake my head a little, but quickly stop when it sends another wave of nausea up from my stomach.

'Just... blood. Can't look at blood. Feel sick.'

'Okay, I'm going to get you a glass of water. I'll be back in a minute. Okay?'

'Yes. Yes,' I say, unable to fully process anything other than trying to keep myself in the here and now.

I focus on my breath. In for five, out for ten, hold for five. Then repeat. Until my racing heart begins to slow and blood returns to my head.

Someone crouches back down next to me and I'm aware of them putting their hand on my arm. 'Here's the water. Can you take a drink?'

After a few moments, I'm able to lift my head and I look round at whoever's next to me.

It's Jonah.

Of course it is.

'You okay?' he asks, his expression concerned.

'Yeah, I'm okay now. Thought I was going to pass out, but... no.'

'You scared me. I thought you were having some sort of fit. You didn't even seem to know your own name and thought you were stuck on an island or something.'

I frown, then suck in a sharp breath as panic sinks through me. *Dammit.* In my dazed state, I'd forgotten I'm supposed to be Dee.

'Um. Sorry, I'm not sure what happened. I was really woozy and disorientated.'

Jonah shakes his head, then presses his mouth into a line. 'Perhaps you should go home?'

'No!' I shake my head, then reach for the glass in his hand. He releases it to me and I take a long, deep drink of water.

'I'm all right now. As long as I don't have to deal with any injuries.' I flash him a sheepish grin.

'Okay. Well, I'm just going to find the medical box for our friend here, then I'll be back to check on you again.'

I nod, then wave a hand towards the poor guy who just came in looking for a plaster and ended up dealing with a fainting woman. 'Sorry about all this,' I say in his general direction, not allowing myself to look at him again in case I catch sight of any more blood.

'No worries. Hope you feel better soon,' he says.

I'm aware of the two of them leaving the room and as soon as the door shuts, I put my head into my hands and groan.

What a wimp! And how embarrassing to have been caught having a funny turn by Jonah.

He returns a few minutes later, by which time, I've got up from the floor and sat with my head between my knees to make sure I'm not going to nearly pass out again.

'How are you doing now?' he asks, approaching where I'm sitting in my office chair.

'Physically, I'm fine. Mentally, I'm in a bit of a state.' I give him an apologetic smile. 'I can't believe I lost the plot like that when I'm supposed to be in charge.'

'Hey, don't beat yourself up about it. It happens.'

'Not to most people,' I point out.

He shrugs. 'No, but it's a real thing. A friend of mine from uni can't see blood without throwing up. There was nothing he could do about it. It's not a failure of character, Dee, if that's what you're worried about?'

'I guess I am.' I frown down at the desk. 'I'd be useless in a medical emergency if someone needed my help and honestly, that really scares me.'

'Sure, but it's unlikely you'd be the only person around to help, right?'

'Yeah, maybe.'

He perches on the edge of my desk and looks down at me with a steady gaze. 'Don't let it get to you. We all have our idio-syncrasies. I know I do.'

His kindness warms me. It suddenly makes him seem so much more human and relatable. He's nothing like the stereo-typical, arrogant, bad-boy rock star I naïvely had him pegged as before I got to know him. I experience a wave of shame about judging him so harshly based on what I'd read on social media.

Looking into his gorgeous, intelligent eyes, which are full of concern, I have to push away another wave of longing.

'What's yours?' I ask to distract myself from my rogue thoughts. I'm also intrigued about what he might admit to. I want to know everything real there is to know about him now.

He cocks an eyebrow and for a second, I think he's going to tell me to mind my own business.

'I dunno. I guess I can be a really grumpy bastard sometimes.'

I can't stop a grin from breaking across my face. 'No kidding.'

'Okay, no need to agree quite so readily,' he says, but the tone of his voice is light and teasing.

'Sorry,' I say with a laugh.

Bless him for attempting to make me feel better. It's not something I would have expected from him.

'I can be upbeat,' he points out. 'It just doesn't come as easily to me as it does to some people. I guess I've always put up this barrier around me,' he swishes his hands through the air in front of him, as if he can touch it, 'and it comes across as aloofness. But I'm not really like that.'

'I'm starting to see that.'

'I can be fun.'

'I know.'

We look at each other for a moment and our gazes lock. His eyes seem to darken as his pupils dilate and I see his expression soften.

A strange sort of buzzy heat rises from my chest up to my throat. Oh no, not again. I really shouldn't be encouraging further closeness with him.

Tearing my gaze away, I stand up from the chair, closing my eyes momentarily as a wave of dizziness descends on me. But I'm okay; it passes quickly.

'Er, perhaps I should go and check on the guy who hurt himself?' I say, deciding I should probably put some distance between myself and Jonah now. His attentiveness is making my good sense wobble.

'No,' Jonah says forcefully. 'He's fine. I dealt with it.'

'Oh. Okay. Great. Well, thanks.'

'Why don't we go out to the fire pit and get you some fresh air for a few minutes. I'm guessing you haven't taken a break for a while?'

'I'm fine. Really. You don't need to look after me.'

'Don't argue. You need a break. Come and have a drink by the fire with me.' He signals for me to follow him out of the room and I realise there's no way I can refuse without seeming either rude or insubordinate.

Sucking in a steadying breath, I follow him down the corridor to the kitchen, where he makes us both a cup of coffee. Handing one to me, he says, 'Right, let's see what we're missing outside.'

I walk with him to the door to the staff exit, my whole body jittery with nerves, and emerge into the fresh air. It's just as noisy out here and we dodge our way through groups of people dotted about the lawns surrounding the house, all chatting animatedly or dancing to the low beat of music coming from the ballroom where a drum and bass DJ is pumping out tunes.

There are solar-powered fairy lights strung from every available surface, including the manicured shrubs and trees next to the house, turning the garden into a Winter Wonderland. Laughter floats over from the hot tubs and I wonder how people can bear to get in and out of them naked in this plummeting temperature.

We turn towards the front of the house where a large fire has been lit in the sunken pit at the end of the terrace. There are usually tables and chairs arranged around it for guests at the hotel to sit and have a drink in the summer months, but right now it's ringed with large blankets, beanbags and cushions. The fire is blazing away with sweet-scented fallen branches which have been gathered from the woods on the estate. The air is crisp and cool, but as soon as we sit down in a space close to the fire, my skin begins to heat from the gentle warmth the fire's giving out.

We sit quietly for a few moments, sipping our coffees and staring into the flames.

'You know,' Jonah says, turning to look at me, 'it's great to see the house come alive like this. The parties I used to hold here in my university holidays were legendary. They got pretty wild. But it's all been a bit sedate around here recently.'

'I imagine they were a lot of fun.'

'Yeah, sometimes. I used to get fifty or more people turning up. Not that I invited them all.' He raises an eyebrow, then looks back at the fire. 'A lot of people were fascinated to visit a house that my dad owned, I think. Not that he ever came here.'

'It must be strange, having a dad that's as famous as he is.'

'I guess I've never found it strange because I grew up with it. But it's definitely been stressful at times. People expect things of you when you come from a family like mine. Things you can't necessarily live up to. As I mentioned the other night, my whole status and success in life has always been tied to and compared with my old man's. Which sucks, because that's a ridiculously high bar to reach.'

It suddenly occurs to me that I might find my father a tough act to follow, but at least I don't have to do it whilst being scrutinised and judged by strangers, then publicly torn down if I fail.

'And some people only want to be associated with you for the reflected glory they think comes with it,' he goes on. 'Especially partners. It turned out Tessa was like that. My ex. Trouble is, that shit can make you paranoid about whether people are sticking around because they genuinely care about you,' he says, his gaze flicking to mine momentarily, before he looks away again. 'I've come to realise over the years that people are perfectly happy to be fake to your face if they think there's something in it for them. I can't stand disingenuous hangers-on.'

I catch the flash of pain on his face and hot guilt rushes through me at the thought that he might consider me to be one of those people right now. I'm not doing it to leech off him though, but to help navigate a messed-up situation for my sister.

And I'm not looking to start a romantic relationship with him either. It sounds like he's not in the market for one anyway, if he's freshly out of a messy break-up.

'But then I felt like I was playing a part a lot of the time with her,' he adds. 'Though I guess most of us would say that about life in general. I just wish people could be straight with each other; it would save us all a lot of pain.'

I can feel my face getting hot as my discomfort about my and Dee's ruse increases. The more I'm getting to know Jonah, the worse I'm feeling about not being entirely honest with him.

'Jay seems really pleased with the way the festival's going, anyway,' I say to change the subject, so I don't get myself caught in any more knots. The more Jonah tells me about himself, the worse I'm going to feel when I have to walk away from him and relay all his secrets to Dee. 'I wouldn't be surprised if he asks to book here for the one he runs in the summer and perhaps hold the winter one here next year too,' I add.

Jonah seems to think about this, still gazing into the flames, then nods. 'All credit to you. Having the festival here was a great idea, but it's not going to be regular enough to keep the place profitable over the off season. We need to work on a more sustainable business model if I'm going to keep it running as a hotel and venue.'

'Can I ask: what were your plans when you first took it over? Other than accommodating guests and weddings here?' I ask. 'And do you have any ideas for the sorts of things you'd like to expand into if you decide not to give the place up?'

'Well, when I first got here, I toyed with the idea of starting a cider-making business on the site. The orchard is already well established and the fruit mostly goes to waste year on year. But I've not had a chance to develop it as an idea yet; I've been too bogged down with running the hotel on my own.'

'Cider? Huh. You know what, that could really work. There's a place quite nearby that's doing that. You should check it out. It's just a bit further into Somerset, near Bruton. The Newt, do you know it?'

'I've heard of it, yeah, but I've never visited.'

'You should. It's wonderful. You could also do tours around the press and hold some tasting sessions. People love to give those sorts of things as birthday experiences. There's lots you could do. There's another boutique hotel quite nearby here – my dad took us there for a meal recently – it's about the same size as this place and it's set up really well. That place would definitely be worth a recon visit if you've not already been.'

'You're just full of good ideas at the moment, aren't you? What's going on? Have you been keeping them all under your hat till now so you can bring them out at the right moment and dazzle me with them?'

'Are you dazzled?' I ask, hoping to divert him from the fact Dee and I clearly have very different approaches to this job.

'A little bit, yeah.'

I shrug. 'Well, I'm just trying to help. I'd hate to see this place fail and I really don't want to lose my job. I like it here,' I say, telling myself I'm channelling Dee right now, so it's not technically lying. It's disseminating information by proxy.

'Yeah. Well, it likes you too. I'm impressed. Really.'

Heat rises to my cheeks. 'Thanks. That's good to hear.'

There's a small pause where we both stare at the dancing flames of the fire.

'Why don't you come with me to that place you were talking about on Monday, once the festival's wrapped up and they've all left?' he says, making me start. 'We can take notes on what they're doing there and start working up a plan for how to emulate it here. I'd really appreciate your thoughts on it.'

'Oh. Er...' I'm desperately trying to think of an excuse, but nothing immediately springs to mind. I'm supposed to be 'twisting my ankle' on Monday morning, to follow Dee's plan for re-integrating when she eventually makes it home, but the idea of spending one more day with Jonah is too much of a lure. I can have my 'accident' in the evening after our trip. 'Yes, okay. That's a great idea,' I say, before I can stop myself.

It's only one more day. And I'd really like to be able to help in any way I can at this point. He's clearly a good guy who's been struggling to keep all his plates spinning on his own.

'Great. Let's plan to meet in the car park at one o'clock. The circus will have left by then, right?'

'Yes, they're aiming to start striking the site first thing and be away by midday. So even if we give them a bit of grace to run over, we should be free to leave by one.'

'Good. It's a date,' His brow creases. 'I mean, that's a plan.'

He stands up and brushes little flakes of ash from the fire off the front of his jumper. 'Right, well I'm going to head back to my place now then. Night.'

'Night,' I say to his retreating figure.

He doesn't turn to look at me again. Instead, he disappears into the darkness, leaving me staring after him, my mind a chaos of conflicting thoughts.

12

JONAH

I keep a low profile on Sunday and don't see Dee at all, leaving her to make sure the festival wraps up successfully.

I'm weirdly nervous about seeing her today though.

Sitting and chatting with her by the fire on Saturday night felt strangely intimate. With the soft light from the flames playing across her gorgeous face and the way we had to lean in close to hear what each other was saying, it once again felt like we had a genuine and unusual connection to each other.

Chemistry.

I regret talking about Tessa now because it seemed to kill the closeness building between us. From the expression on her face, Dee was clearly uncomfortable discussing something as personal as the breakdown of my last relationship. But seeing her looking so vulnerable after nearly passing out, I'd wanted to let her into my head. To show her I have vulnerabilities too. To remind her there are genuine reasons for me being the grumpy bastard she has me pegged as, after my less than friendly behaviour towards her.

No wonder she's pushing me away now though. She must be totally confused about what I'm all about when I've been so hot and cold with her.

I feel like I still barely know anything about her and I have to admit, I'm intrigued. I'd like to know what makes her tick.

Her reluctance to let me in is actually more of a turn on than when she out and out flirted with me.

As Dee predicted, the whole festival is wrapped and packed up by midday and as she'd promised, you wouldn't even know it had happened, apart from a few large patches of flattened grass where the marquees and tents had been, which will spring back in no time.

It's an impressive operation that her friend, Jay's running and I have to admit, I'd be more than happy for him to use the place to host his events in the future. It could turn out to be quite a lucrative thing if we manage to come to an arrangement about fees for the hire of the place, especially if he's wanting to book out a long weekend in high season as well.

I'm really buzzed by the idea of it. I loved seeing the place being used to its fullest and I've had a lot of people approach me to say thanks and tell me how much they've enjoyed being in the hotel. It made a real change from people coming over to ask for a selfie or to tell me how much they love my dad. And it warmed my soul to be complimented on something I'd brought to fruition outside of my family's fame. Something I'd achieved as me, rather than my father's son.

Hopefully, the interest shown in the hotel might actually translate into more room bookings in the future too, especially if they go on to tell all their friends and family about the place.

It's heart-warming to hear that other people love the house and grounds as much as I do.

For the first time in a long time, I feel proud again to be the guardian of the place.

I'm excited to plan what else we can do with it.

It occurs to me that I haven't felt this level of excitement about the future in ages and a lot of that is down to Dee. It's uplifting to be around her positivity. Infectious.

And the return of my enthusiasm for the project is most welcome.

On that note, at one o'clock on the dot, I see Dee coming out of the staff entrance to the house and make her way over to where I'm waiting for her by my car, ready to take the trip to the boutique hotel she mentioned yesterday.

It's a great idea to scope out competitors, something I've not done in this area yet. I know I should have undergone more research before launching into running a hotel myself, but I was too excited to get stuck in and Tessa never seemed interested in coming along with me to look at places, so I just kept letting it slide. Looking back now, I can see how naïve I was to think I could just launch into this business without doing the research or having the experience needed to make it a success. But I guess I was so hell-bent on proving to myself and to everyone else – particularly my dad, if I'm honest – that I could make it work on my own merit and without help from anyone else.

That I'm more than just a pale imitation of him.

What a short-sighted idiot I was.

No wonder the hotel's been struggling. With Dee's help, insight and intelligent ideas, I have a good feeling about turning the place into a going concern now though.

And I'm looking forward to being inspired today. It's about time I felt something other than despair and lethargy towards the project I was once so excited to get my teeth into.

Perhaps we can visit some of the cider-making businesses later in the week too. I was heartened to hear she thought it would be a good idea to start a press here. It's something I've been toying with for a while and the more I think about it, the more enthusiasm I have for the idea.

But one step at a time.

'Hi,' Dee says as she reaches me. 'Ready for our research trip?' She gives me a grin which makes me think she's not feeling the same worries about the state of things between us as I am, which is a relief. I really don't want to mess up the relationship we're tentatively building between us. I'd hate to lose her now.

'Absolutely. Let's go.' I open the passenger door for her and motion for her to get in. She does so with a nod of thanks.

Walking round to the driver's seat, I roll back my shoulders, trying to trick my body into relaxing.

It's a fool's errand, of course, because as soon as I slide into my seat next to her and her familiar sweet scent hits my senses, my cock's immediately back on high alert.

She must sense my agitation because she turns to me and asks, 'Everything okay?'

I force myself to smile at her. 'Fine,' I say. 'All good.'

But it's really not.

* * *

We spend the twenty-minute journey east chatting about our favourite parts of the festival.

I love hearing the passion in her voice as she talks about the workshops that most caught her imagination.

Notably, the lube wrestling isn't mentioned.

'You know, holding the festival at the hotel reminded me why

I love the place so much and why I wanted to be able to share it with other people,' I say.

I feel her looking at me and when I glance over, I see she's smiling, waiting for me to go on.

So I do. 'I love how it has the potential to bring people together – to give them a platform for adventure, whatever that translates to.' I shake my head. 'Ugh! Listen to me, I sound like a cheesy bloody inspirational quote.'

'No, no! I like it,' she says, with real warmth in her voice. 'We could use the essence of what you're saying in our marketing campaign.'

'The essence. How very tactful of you.'

She just laughs at my gruffness and I can't help but smile back.

A minute later, the sign for the hotel appears and I turn into the driveway and follow it past lush, green lawns and into the visitors' car park.

This hotel isn't dissimilar in style to Gladbrooke House and I can see exactly why Dee thought it'd be helpful for me to come and visit. It has the same type of Bath-stone façade and extensive grounds, which are immaculately kept.

As we walk towards the front entrance, she puts her hand onto my arm, urging me to stop for a moment.

'I hope this is okay: I called ahead this morning and told them we're thinking about hiring the hotel for our wedding venue and that we'd like to take a look around,' she says in a low voice.

Her cheeks are pink and she's having trouble looking me in the eye. 'I thought it would be useful to see one of their luxury rooms, as well as the spa and the other facilities and I didn't think it'd be wise to sneak around in case we got caught. I gave them fake names so hopefully they won't twig we're from a rival hotel.' She takes a breath. 'What I didn't consider was that they might recognise you, so you might need to pretend you just look like Jonah Jacobson or something and that you hear that comparison all the time. Sorry to put you in that position.'

I nod, my mouth lifting at the corner at her obvious discomfort at asking me to tell a white lie. Or is it because we're going to have to act like an engaged couple?

'Yeah, no problem,' I say, and I see her visibly relax.

I, on the other hand, am anything but relaxed.

'Okay, so otherwise, are you happy for me to do most of the talking?'

'The lying, you mean?' I joke, but I'm alarmed to see her face fall.

She shifts on her feet. 'I like to think of it more as play-acting because we're not going to hurt anyone with our ruse. And I booked us in for afternoon tea, so we'll be paying our way.'

Her voice is plaintive, as if asking for my blessing, or perhaps my forgiveness.

'Er, yeah, sure. I didn't mean to suggest anything by that. I'm not calling you a liar. You don't strike me as the type to take advantage of people.'

If anything, my response increases the look of tension on her face.

'Are you okay?' I ask, worried now. 'We don't have to do this if it's too stressful. We can just go in for afternoon tea and take a cursory look around afterwards.'

Dee clears her throat and seems to give herself a mental shake. 'No, no. Let's do it. It'll be helpful to see the whole set up. That's what we're here for, after all.' Her professional self is fully back in place now and she looks me directly in the eye this time, her expression assured. 'Okay.'

'Okay then, fiancée. Let's take a look around our wedding venue.'

She grins at this and gives a jerky nod.

Instinctively, I reach out my hand, offering to take hers, then check myself, realising this is probably a bad idea and withdraw it again.

She's noticed the gesture though and gives a little frown as if worried she didn't respond quickly enough and has offended me.

'Forget it,' I say. 'I just thought for a second that it'd look more convincing, but we don't need to.'

'No. You're right,' she says, her mouth forming a determined line. 'It's a good idea.' She reaches out and slides her hand into mine, smiling up at me.

My heart turns over and my skin prickles where our fingers link. The sensation travels up my arm to my throat, where a rapid pulse begins to throb.

Yeah, this wasn't such a good idea. What was I thinking? The last thing I need to be doing is touching her right now. I'm having a hard enough time as it is keeping my mind on the practical reason for being here and not how she's making my pulse race.

Seeming not to notice my apprehension, she begins walking again towards the reception to the hotel, which is housed in one of the rooms off the main entrance. Once there, she charms the friendly events co-ordinator, who thankfully doesn't seem to recognise me. The hotel is quiet, so we barely see anyone else – and those people we do see don't give us a second glance – as she proceeds to lead us on a tour, showing us the bar area and lounges, in beautifully appointed rooms which have light pouring in through large picture windows, before taking us outside and onto the patio with its outdoor kitchen and terrace.

It's refreshing to feel like a normal person doing normal things. When I was with Tessa, she would insist on making sure everyone knew who we were and that we expected special treatment because of it. I found it excruciating at times, so not having to put on an act here is a relief and I start to relax and actually enjoy myself as the tour continues and Dee chats animatedly with our host.

She leads us next to the spa, pointing out the heated outdoor pool, which has a large hot tub adjacent to it, with views out over the fields. The spa itself has an indoor pool, steam rooms, a gym and treatment rooms, all well-kept and immaculately decorated. Throughout the tour, Dee keeps hold of my hand, giving it a small covert squeeze whenever she sees something that seems to particularly interest her. This place is set up much better than Gladbrooke at the moment, but the inspiration it's stirring in me shoots thrills of excitement through my veins.

This is exactly what I want to be aiming for with my hotel and it feels great to be finally giving plans for the future the attention they deserve.

Outside the main entrance to the spa, she finally drops my hand – leaving me a little bereft at the sudden loss of contact – and we walk through a courtyard planted with well-established plants and flower beds, past a rack of bicycles available for guests to borrow, then over a large, striped lawn with a huge circle marked out on the grass. I wonder for a second what it's there for, then I see that there's the letter H in the middle of it.

'It's a helipad for guests travelling here in helicopters,' our tour guide tells us.

I turn to Dee and she raises her eyebrows at me at the exact same time I do it to her.

We grin at each other, enjoying the shared moment.

I love that she seems to instinctively know what I'm thinking.

'Very cool,' Dee murmurs.

'If you'll follow me, we'll walk round to one of the luxury

suites where the bride and groom would normally stay,' she says, beckoning us to follow her.

We stroll around to the far side of the hotel, past tennis courts – in a much better state than the ones at Gladbrooke are currently in – to some newer-looking cottages. As we walk in through a gateway set into a gap in the hedge, which gives the rooms privacy from the rest of the site, I see an outdoor bath sitting under one of the windows, then as we walk around the corner, there's a hot tub for the exclusive use of the suite.

'Nice,' I say, widening my eyes at Dee.

She nods back and smiles. 'This is wonderful,' she murmurs to me.

'And here's the suite,' the hotelier says, unlocking the door and opening it, motioning for us to go inside.

It's a beautifully appointed room, decorated in greens and pinks, with swathes of fabric scooped across the ceiling, giving one the impression of being inside a large, luxurious tent.

'The bathroom has a steam room in it and there's a massage table in case you fancy a treatment while you're staying with us,' she adds.

We walk into the bathroom, which is palatial. The shower cubicle is huge and has a tiled bench in it where guests sit to steam themselves.

'Wow,' Dee says, widening her eyes at me.

'I'll leave you to look around for a few minutes if you like,' our guide tells us. 'Just pull the door closed behind you when you're done.'

'Thank you,' Dee says, smiling at her.

She gives us one last friendly nod and leaves us there alone.

'This place is amazing!' Dee whispers, her voice full of awe.

'It sure is. I love all the luxury touches,' I say, 'and the lighting design is fantastic.' I point to the huge, designer light pendants which are made up of circles intertwined with each other.

There's a moment where we just look at each other, perhaps thinking about what it would be like to be actually staying here. Together? At least that's what I'm thinking.

I allow myself to imagine for a second what it would feel like to pull her towards me and kiss her. To taste her. To explore her body with my mouth...

I clear my throat and walk out of the bathroom and back into the main room, my eyes drawn to the huge bed. I have to tear my gaze away from it as I feel her follow me out and come to stand next to me.

The air seems to be pulsing around me, as if my need for her has a life of its own and is escaping into the air around us.

Oh man, I have to get out of here. Away from temptation.

She seems to sense my agitation because she says, 'Jonah?' in such a way, I suspect she's thinking the exact same thing as me. Her eyes are wide and her pupils large and dark against her irises as she stares into mine.

But is she? Can she be feeling this irrevocable pull between us and the drive to give in to it that I am? Surely not after what she said to me the other day about maintaining our roles.

'Are you hungry?'

The flash of warmth I see in her eyes is welcome, but I don't smile back. If I do, I'll lose it completely and I'm determined to remain professional around her. I promised her I would, after all. And she's right about us setting those boundaries. I'm her boss, so it wouldn't be a good idea to cross that line.

Even though the restraint I'm clinging on to feels tenuous at best.

'Yep,' I say stiffly.

For more than you know.

'Okay. Let's eat,' she says, breaking the intense eye contact between us and leading the way out of the suite.

I'm glad now that she's walking in front of me down the narrow path, so she can't see my frown of concentration as I try to will my deviant cock to calm the hell down.

In the restaurant, we're shown to our table and she gestures for me to take the seat with the view across the large front garden, where a few people are braving the cool weather to play croquet on the lawn.

Our waiter takes our coats and tells us what to expect from the afternoon tea that Dee's ordered for us.

'We'll take one glass of champagne as well,' I tell the waiter, who smiles and nods before retreating, leaving us on our own.

'You're in need of a drink, are you?' Dee says with a small smile. 'I hope it's not my company that's driving you to it.'

I let out a snort of laughter. 'Actually, it's for you.'

'Oh!'

'To say thanks for all the hard work you put into hosting the festival at such short notice. I know it was long hours and I'm grateful for how much effort you put into making it a success.'

Colour has risen to her cheeks at my compliment. 'Well, it was my absolute pleasure. I really enjoyed it.'

'It looked like it.'

She's smiling, but her eyes don't meet mine.

We're interrupted by the waiter returning with her drink.

'Thank you,' she says again, taking a small sip. 'You're not indulging too?'

'No. I'm off booze at the moment,' I say.

She doesn't press me on this, which I'm grateful for.

The waiter re-appears with a three-tiered cake stand filled with delicious-looking sandwiches, mini cakes and scones and places it between us on the table.

'This looks amazing,' Dee says with real pleasure in her voice. She's such an upbeat person to be around, I realise. Whenever I'm with her, she's nothing but positive about the things going on around her. It's refreshing after the crap I went through with Tessa, who was very difficult to impress.

'You have a really great attitude, you know, so positive,' I tell her, deciding to let her in on what's going on in my mind. I've always been really bad at thinking good things but not saying them aloud to the people I'm with, but Dee's inspiring me to be more open with my feelings.

'Oh, thanks,' she says, choosing a sandwich and putting it on her plate. 'I guess I've trained myself to be that way. Growing up, both my parents were really negative – especially towards each other – and I've been determined not to fall into acting that way myself.'

'Sorry to hear that. Are they still together?'

'No. They got divorced when we were twelve.'

'Ugh. That's a tough age to have your family ripped apart. At least mine were never married and barely even lived together because of my dad's touring so it didn't feel like much of a change when they split.'

'That's good,' she says, biting into her sandwich and making a face of pure pleasure.

I have to look away as my entire body reacts to it.

'So, did you and your sister live with your mum or your dad?' I ask her, to distract myself from the desire that's now rushing through my veins.

'We split our time between both to begin with, but eventually I ended up living mostly with my dad while... my sister lived with my mum. She moved into this artsy sort of commune, which was always messy and full of people and I found it really wearing. Especially when I was trying to do my homework.'

I start to work my way through the sandwiches as she talks, suddenly realising how hungry I am.

'Mum has a really hands-off approach to parenting, the complete opposite to our dad, which I found difficult. I'm an independent sort of person, but sometimes you just need your mum to be the adult, you know? But most of the time, it felt like I was parenting her.'

'And your sister?' I ask.

Dee seems to pause for a moment and stare at the plate of cakes, the colour returning to her cheeks again. Perhaps it's the champagne that's bringing about both the flush and the chattiness. Whatever it is, I like it.

'Um, well, she kind of likes doing her own thing so it suited her better to live with my mum.' She picks up a scone and stabs the middle of it with her knife, slicing it into two perfect halves before slathering them both with cream and jam. 'Did you go on tour much with your dad?' she asks, still not looking at me.

I finish eating the cake I've just stuffed into my mouth and shake my head. 'Nah. Not often anyway. My brother and I were at boarding school most of the time. I went along to a few gigs in my late teens, mostly for the party scene afterwards, but I barely spent any time with the old man. He's never really been that interested in being a parent either. I spent most of my childhood trying to get his attention, without success. He's always just treated us like mini adults, letting us do whatever the hell we wanted, as long as we didn't get in his face. And if we did, it usually resulted in him paying someone else to deal with it.'

Dee nods and takes one of the small cakes from the plate now and pops it into her mouth, her brows drawn together as she chews. Once she's swallowed it, she says, 'Yeah, it's the same sort of story with my mum – apart from the paying-off thing. She has very little patience for anything that isn't about her and her art. I can see why she and my dad got divorced, to be honest; they're polar opposites of each other.'

'Just like you and your sister, from the sounds of it.'

'Yeah.' Dee takes a gulp of champagne, then bangs the flute down and says, 'So, anyway, enough about me. Perhaps we could go for a walk around the grounds before we head back?' She picks up her champagne glass again with what looks like a trembling hand then raises it to her lips and tips the last drops of liquid into her mouth, before replacing it with studied carefulness this time onto the table and gesturing for the waitress to bring our bill.

I'm a bit confused by her sudden abruptness and apparent need to leave the restaurant when we were having such an interesting conversation. But then, perhaps she feels it's getting too personal again for her liking.

The waiter brings the bill and I pay it before Dee has a chance to offer. 'It's a business expense,' I tell her forcibly.

'Oh, okay. Great,' she says with a warm smile. The champagne has given her eyes a real sparkle and I experience another rush of longing to lean over and kiss her.

Instead, I stand up from my chair and signal for the waiting staff to bring out coats, which they do quickly.

She leads the way out of the restaurant, then the hotel, thanking all the staff she encounters on her way out.

We head away from the hotel and across the lawn towards where the person on reception told us the river is.

'What do you think of this place?' she asks as we stride purposefully down the hill.

'It's terrific. Food for thought.'

'Right?'

'Yeah. Lots of things to think about. This place makes me realise that Gladbrooke has a lot of untapped potential.'

'It really does. It's crying out for an upgrade.'

'Yeah. There's just the small matter of finding the funds to do it.'

'Hmm.' She stares thoughtfully down at the ground.

'I guess I could try and persuade my dad to hold off on selling the place for a bit longer and try and get a loan from the bank to do the refurbishments. I'll need to put a business proposal together for it though, so I can be confident I can pay it back once the hotel's up and running properly. I've been reluctant to do that up till now because... well, I guess I didn't want to do it on my own.'

There's something a little sad in the smile she gives me when I turn to look at her, or perhaps it's wariness.

'You don't think I should do that?' I ask.

She shakes her head. 'No, no, I do. It'd be a shame not to. It could be a really profitable venture.'

'Yeah. We just need to get the level of luxury right.'

'And use its natural assets. You have that wonderful lake. You could get some rowing boats and hire them out to guests. Perhaps arrange picnics for them to have on the bank in good weather. And put up a pagoda to hold wedding ceremonies in, maybe.'

Bad memories rush back into my head and I give a shudder.

She frowns. 'Too twee?'

I shake my head. 'No, no, nothing like that. It's just... I hate the idea of returning to the scene of the crime.'

When I glance at her, I see her nose is wrinkled. 'What crime? Did I miss something? Was there a death there or something?'

'Only the death of my reputation,' I try to joke, but it falls flat.

She blinks at me, appearing confused. 'Sorry, I don't get what you mean.'

I stop and turn to stare at her. I thought everyone in the country had witnessed my humiliation. I'd have thought Dee would definitely know about it. She seems pretty social media savvy. But from the look on her face, I'm guessing it's somehow passed her by.

'You mean you didn't see the meme?' I ask incredulously. 'I thought the entire human race had seen it. It certainly felt like that the weeks after it went viral.'

'I'm afraid I didn't,' she says.

I'm really surprised by this, but I can hear the clear ring of truth in her voice, so I know she's not taking the piss.

'The way Tessa and I broke up?'

'Nope. Sorry. You're going to have to fill me in.'

'You don't want to hear this shit.'

'I really do. Please. Tell me.'

From the expression on her face, it seems she means it too and she's not going to let me get away with brushing it to one side.

I sigh, wishing I'd kept my mouth shut now. But there's no point keeping it from her; she's bound to find out at some point from someone else. And I'd much rather she heard the full truth about it from me.

'You know those romcoms where the audience knows that the girl's with the wrong guy at the start of the movie but she spends the whole time kidding herself she really does want to be with him, even though he's clearly a loser?'

'Yeah, my sister, De-Beatrice has made me watch a few of those with her. They're not really my bag though.'

'Then at the end, the guy she's meant to be with all along crashes some big important event and proclaims his love to her in some vomit-inducing grand gesture and she falls into his arms and everyone breathes a sigh of relief that she's finally made the right choice?'

'Yeah...'

'Well, I'm the loser in that scenario.'

'What? What are you talking about? You can't be.'

'And yet that's exactly what happened with me and my ex.'

'You're kidding, right?'

'Nope. At least that's the narrative she's made famous on her social media channels.' I rub my hand over my hair, then look at her with a rueful expression. 'I keep asking myself how the fuck I became that guy.'

'You don't know?'

'Well, yeah. I do. Through poor judgement and a certain degree of self-importance.'

She shoots me a confused frown and I realise I'm going to have to tell her the whole sorry tale now. I can't just leave it at that.

And the thing is, I want to. Because, instinctively, I trust her. I don't believe she'll hold it against me. It just doesn't seem in her nature to do that. She's too kind.

So, I let out a long, low sigh and let it all flow out of me.

'I met Tessa at a party backstage after one of my band's gigs, about three years ago. We were just starting to break through and things were going well for us. She was often at the muso parties I went to, so I'd seen her around a lot. She was a real party girl, always the centre of attention in any group. She's a beautiful woman and she really knows it. Famous for being famous, one of those types. When I met her, she'd just started to get traction as an influencer on social media and a high-profile spirits company were starting to sponsor her posts. She was absolutely in her element. As was I. I'd been on a real high about becoming a professional musician before the press – then everyone else –

began to tear me down, but after months and months of bad reviews and a lot of shit posts about me and how untalented I am appearing regularly on social media, it all began to wear a bit thin. I got pretty depressed about it, to be honest. It had been the first time in my life I'd felt as if I was doing something of some worth, but I wasn't allowed to enjoy it.

'I started drinking and partying hard. And a lot. Tessa came along for the ride with me, which wasn't great because we just enabled each other. It got so bad, I started turning up to gigs absolutely shit-faced and couldn't play. So the band kicked me out. That was the point I realised I needed to change something in my life. It turned out it was the dream of being a musician. It brought me nothing but trouble. In the end, I realised I wasn't cut out for a career in the music industry. I was never going to equal my old man. So I took the decision to step away and not perform in public any more.

'I spun out after that and ended up in rehab. My dad offered to let me stay and recover at Gladbrooke and I got really attached to the place again. So when he decided to sell the house, I had the bright idea of taking it on and running it as a boutique hotel. It felt like an opportunity for a fresh start and the chance at a new direction in life. Not that I had any experience in being a hotelier. At all. Tessa wasn't exactly delighted by the idea either. She wanted to be the girlfriend of a rock star, or the lauded son of one of the most famous rock stars in the world, I guess. That was great for her profile. But being the girlfriend of a depressed hotelier, not so much.'

I flash Dee a rueful grin, but she presses her mouth into a hard line and shakes her head.

I'm grateful for her understanding. The humiliation of what happened has hung around me like a bad smell for so long, it's great to finally start feeling like I'm shaking it off.

'As soon as I made the decision to give up being a musician, she started to lose interest in me. But she came along to Gladbrooke, albeit reluctantly. I thought she was actually up for giving this new lifestyle a go with me at first. That she loved me enough to try, at least.'

I tear my gaze away and stare straight ahead, hoping she won't notice the heat flooding my face. This is really hard to talk about, but surprisingly, I feel okay telling Dee about it. I don't think she'll go and blab the whole thing to other people.

'It came to a head when she started documenting our life, but flat-out lying about a lot of what we were doing and how solid our relationship was. I really wasn't into the idea of being involved in that. I was resistant to being in photos anyway, especially when she was advertising things. It didn't sit well with me. I'm actually a very private person when it comes to my personal life, and I'm especially sensitive after all the shit the press wrote about me when I was partying and performing, so I wasn't keen on putting my life out there for people to scrutinise.

'This really frustrated Tessa though. She used to get angry with me and accuse me of trying to sabotage her livelihood. I have to admit, I wasn't happy about what she did for a living. I find the whole influencer thing really objectionable. The falseness of it grates on me. But it was her career, so I put up with it.'

We reach the river and I gesture for us to sit down on the grassy bank. She nods and sits, wrapping her arms around her knees and waits for me to continue with my story.

I flop down next to her and stare off across to the other side of the bank, where a mature weeping willow dips its branches into the slow-flowing water.

'Things hadn't been going well between us for a while by then. I'd become aware of her distancing herself and she started making threats about leaving so, in a drunken moment of madness, I asked her to marry me, stupidly thinking it would make her more willing to stay and give the hotel more of a go with me if she felt secure in our relationship. Before that, I'd been really against marriage. It was the main thing we'd argued about. She wanted it; I didn't. Anyway, this seemed to placate her and she treated it like a real marriage proposal and accepted.'

I shrugged. 'So that was it. We were engaged. She spent ages organising this big, flashy engagement party down by the lake. I thought when she suggested it that it'd be a small gathering of close friends, but Tessa had pretty much invited her entire social media friends list, which I was pretty pissed off about. She was clearly making it into an event she could use to promote herself online with, rather than it being about the two of us celebrating with the people we cared about.'

I glance at Dee and see she's pulling a face of antipathy at this. Her support gives me a warm feeling in my chest, which allows me to continue.

'What I didn't know was that she was cheating on me the whole time with the guy who ran her social-media campaign that paid her as an influencer, who also happens to be the son of a famous actor. When we first moved to Gladbrooke, she convinced me to hire him as our events and marketing manager, so he was always around.'

I shrug, aiming for nonchalance, but I'm aware of how tense I am and it must look really awkward to her because she shoots me a look of horror.

I quickly turn away to stare blindly at the water flowing past us, fighting back the sinking feeling of humiliation that's plagued me for months. 'Anyway, Jack, the events guy, turned up as we were having some photos taken in front of the lake. He was clearly really drunk and barged his way into the party. I could see Tessa was uncomfortable with him being there and I stupidly just assumed it was because he was an employee and hadn't been invited. Anyway, not long after arriving, he came storming over to us, where we were standing in front of the lake. I was in the middle of refusing to have any more photos taken – we'd been there for bloody ages and the photographer must have taken hundreds already – so I was acting a bit grumpy with Tessa.' I raise my eyebrows at Dee, letting her know I realise I was out of order being like that at my own engagement party.

'Really? That doesn't sound like you,' Dee says, deadpan, then shooting me a teasing smile.

I grunt, then smile back at her. I like the way she handles my grouchiness. She has a lovely way of batting it away without taking it to heart. Something Tessa was never able to do. She took everything to heart, as if everyone else's bad moods were a personal insult aimed directly at her.

'The grumpier I got about the photos, the angrier and more aggressive he seemed to get, shouting comments like, "At least try to look like you're pleased to be engaged to her," at me. I didn't understand what was going on at first. I thought he was pissed off that I wasn't taking the photoshoot seriously. I could sense Tessa getting upset and I stupidly thought it was because he was being such a dickhead and ruining our party by being so drunk, but then she broke away from the shoot to take him to one side, away from everyone. I could tell from her body language and tone of voice that she wasn't angry with him; she was actually trying to calm him down and placate him about something. I guess I kind of knew it then, in the back of my mind. They'd always been really chummy and flirty around each other, with little "in jokes" between them, from the very first time I saw them together. But I'd ignored it, convincing myself she wouldn't cheat on me. Not with him. That she genuinely loved me. Pure arrogance, on my part.'

'Don't be so hard on yourself. That doesn't sound like arrogance. Just having faith in someone you cared about.'

'Hmm, yeah maybe. Anyway, the longer she talked to him, touching his arm and staring intently into his eyes, the more worked up I got, till I'd had enough and went over to where they were standing and demanded to know what the hell was going on. I wasn't exactly subtle about how frustrated I was with the two of them and they both turned on me as if I was the one making trouble. Tessa told me to leave them alone, that she just needed a minute to work something out with Jack. He's even got a hero's name. Fucker. But I'd had enough by then and told her to ignore him, that he wasn't even invited and he should fuck off and leave us alone. And that's when he rushed at me and shoved me – hard – so I stumbled backwards and nearly fell on my ass. I saw red and was advancing towards him when Tessa told me to leave him the hell alone. I was so stunned that she was defending him, it stopped me in my tracks. And that's when he told me – and the entire gathering of gawping onlookers, including all my friends and family – that he was in love with her and she was in love with him, not me. That they'd been having an affair for months and she felt trapped by me and the situation that I'd "forced her into". Which was bullshit, by the way. I'd never made her do a thing. She chose to move here with me, even if she regretted it afterwards. Clearly, she was just humouring me about making the hotel work and was waiting for me to come to my senses and move back to London. I guess at first she was just whiling away her time with Jack, until it became clear he was the better bet and she could capitalise on the drama between us all. They're quite the power couple now, apparently, after their social-media status skyrocketed post Darcy meme.'

'Hmm. It's funny,' Dee says. 'You don't always get to know the real person till they're forced into something they have to fight against – or for.'

'Yeah. I was blinded by her effortless cool. Tessa was an exciting person to be around. She's one of those people that make things happen. You know the type?'

'Yeah, I do.'

'I guess she reminded me of the fun I used to have at my uni parties at the house. I stupidly thought a combo of her and the house would be amazing, but it turned out they cancelled each other out.'

We sit quietly for a moment, both staring off across the water. The whole side of my body next to her is prickling with awareness.

'So what happened after Jack accused you of trapping her?'

I take a steadying breath, the memory of that awful day making adrenaline surge through my veins. 'I saw the moment she made up her mind about which of us to take sides with. And which she was happy to shame.'

I scuff my shoes against the ground, not able to look at her now. She doesn't say anything, just lets me talk. Now I've finally started to, it's all pouring out of me, as if it's been trapped inside me for too long and I can't stop it.

'I'd never been so humiliated in my life. I felt totally alone, like I'd been made to look a laughing stock in every way possible. So I lost my rag. I stormed towards him, in what must have looked like a really menacing way, and he responded by aiming a punch at me, but missing me completely; I think he was too drunk to have landed anything at that point anyway. I swung back at him in retaliation, catching him right on the nose, and he went down. I'm not proud of it. I shouldn't have done it, I know that, but I was so fucking angry. I was in a blind rage. Anyway, Tessa was right there at his side, checking he was okay and when she saw I'd broken his nose, she went mad. She got up, yelling at me that I was a bully and a gaslighter and that she'd never loved me, that Jack was right, I'd tricked her into something she'd never wanted.'

I take a shuddery breath deep into my lungs. 'I told her she was a crazy bitch – again, I'm not proud of using those words. Totally unacceptable.' I rub my hand over my face in agitation.

'That's when she ran at me and shoved me hard in the chest. I lost my footing and stumbled backwards into the lake. The water was freezing, but even worse, she'd pushed me into a really shallow, muddy bit, so when I resurfaced, I looked like a bloody swamp monster. I was so furious by this point, I resembled something from a horror movie emerging from its dark lair. And the reason I know this is because one of Tessa's friends filmed the whole thing on their mobile and in the aftermath of this entire shitshow, Tessa and Jack edited it into a meme where I call her a "crazy bitch" and she pushes me into the mud in retaliation. They plastered it all over her social media to the delight of her hundreds of thousands of followers. A "Reverse Darcy" they called it, referencing that scene in the *Pride and Prejudice* BBC drama where Darcy comes out of the water looking like a hot hero. According to the internet, I personify the exact opposite of that. It was everywhere, that meme, for ages. I couldn't leave the house without someone shouting that fucking catchphrase at me. So I just stayed at home and drank and let everything go to hell. Till Harry staged an intervention and forced me to get sober. And just as I was getting back on my feet, I hired you. And thank God I did. You've really helped me get back on track with what I've wanted to do with the place. It feels much more *possible* again now. So thanks for that.'

I look at her now, wondering what sort of expression I'm going to see on her face. I'm hoping hard that it's not pity.

It's not.

She's smiling at me, like she gets where I'm coming from. That she gets *me*.

Incredibly, I think telling Dee about what happened with Tessa has taken the sting out of it and the pain I've been carrying around with me since she left seems to have dissipated a little.

'You're most welcome,' she says, her voice full of warmth.

We stare at each other for a little longer than colleagues should.

My heartbeat picks up and I feel it thumping away in my chest.

There's a moment where I think she's going to say something else and I hold my breath, hoping it's that she's changed her mind about wanting to kiss me again.

My gaze automatically drops to her beautiful mouth and I have to forcibly wrench it away and look back into her eyes.

Her pupils are blown and she blinks rapidly, like she's trying to hold something back.

The air between us is heavy with possibility.

God, I really fucking want her. I know I shouldn't, but I can't stop these feelings surfacing, no matter how hard I try.

Dee suddenly breaks eye contact and I jump a little as she slaps her hands onto her thighs then starts to get up. 'I guess we ought to get back.' There's an expression on her face that I can't read now. Is it confusion? Frustration? Or is she just tired of my company? Did I go too far giving her a blow-by-blow of my break-up with Tessa?

I want to ask her what's going through her head, but something in her manner warns me not to. It's as if she's decided we've concluded everything we need to deal with here and now and she's keen to get back.

My heart sinks. I was having such a good time with her and

was actually feeling better after talking to her about all my shit with Tessa.

But I guess I went too far.

She's not my counsellor; she's my colleague.

So, it really is time to go.

We walk in silence back to the car park, get into the car and I drive away without us exchanging another word.

It seems we're both out of conversation now.

And I'm not sure why, but this feels like the end of something.

13

BEATRICE

The journey back to Gladbrooke is painful.

I'm intensely aware that this might be the last time I ever see Jonah and it's all I can do to hold back the hot tears that are threatening to spill out of my eyes.

We don't talk, just sit quietly next to each other as the scenery flies by.

My whole body is jangly with tension and sadness.

I can't believe I have to walk away from this now. From him. Especially as he's just let himself be so vulnerable with me by telling me such personal things.

Sitting and listening to him by that river, I desperately wanted to put my arms around him and hold him close, to tell him he's braver than he knows for battling on, despite the cruelty and setbacks he's had to deal with. But I knew I couldn't do that. It would have led to something I really shouldn't be contemplating.

I'm intensely aware I've let things go too far. I should never have allowed him to confide in me like that, not when I'm pretending to be someone I'm not. He's already experienced so much betrayal and if he finds out about our ruse now, it's going to really hurt him.

How can I fix this? And is that even possible? Will he really believe that Dee is the woman he talked to so candidly by the river?

Hot shame rushes through me.

And if we do get away with it, what if Jonah and Dee get together once she comes back? How am I going to be able to act like I don't mind? That I'm not attracted to him myself? How will I cope, seeing them together, wanting him to be with me instead? But of course, I'm being an idiot. He can't ever know about me. It'll be so obvious the moment he meets me that we've been tricking him.

Oh God. What have I done?

Too soon, we pull in through the gates to the estate and Jonah drives down the winding driveway and pulls into his usual space in the staff car park.

We both get out and walk to the back of the car.

Jonah clears his throat and I force myself to look at him.

He's so gorgeous, with his strong jawline dusted with stubble and his dark, brooding features and my heart soars at the sight. In a frustrating counterpoint, there's also a tightness in my chest that just won't go away. I feel so connected to him now. There's always been something there between us – something intense and exciting – I know that, even though I've been fighting it. I've felt so alive, being around him. Like he's brought technicolour to my formerly monochrome life.

'Well, feel free to head home,' he says. 'It's been a crazy weekend and you deserve some rest. In fact, why don't you take tomorrow off and I'll see you the day after.'

My stomach lurches. I'm going to have to tell him more lies soon. 'Oh, er, yes okay. I guess I could do that. Thanks.'

The sun is low in the sky now and we probably only have about half an hour till it sets.

It feels portentous.

So, this is how it ends.

I turn to go.

'Actually, before you go, could I quickly show you the apple orchard?' he says, as if he wants to delay me leaving.

I really should go, but the hope in his eyes is making it really difficult.

I can't leave. Not this place. Not Jonah. Not yet.

I want to stretch out these last moments with him.

'It'll be good to show you the land around it, for the business proposal I'll need to write for the loan. I'd like to get your thoughts on it. I'm excited about it. I think I'll start writing it tonight.'

'Umm—' I hedge, at a total loss about what to do. I want to be able to help him, but I really should leave.

'Please?' he asks. 'It'll just take a couple of minutes.'

My resolve breaks. I can't leave now. It would seem churlish.

'Okay, sure,' I say.

'Let's not walk that way though,' he says as I start moving away from the house.

'Past the lake, you mean?'

'Exactly. I can barely look at the place now, which really sucks, because I've always loved it down there.'

I feel a rush of anger on his behalf. That bloody woman and her ego has a lot to answer for.

'That's such a shame. Are you really going to let that one memory stop you from going there again?'

'It just feels wrong now. Tainted, or something.'

I badly want to do something to make him feel better about it all, but I'm not sure what. He clearly needs to purge this humiliation so he can get past it. It seems to be haunting him. Perhaps holding him back from moving on with his life.

'Hey, you know what you should do?' I say.

'What?' he asks a little warily, though there's a flash of something bright and hopeful in his eyes.

'You should make a new happy memory there.'

The brightness in his gaze intensifies.

'What sort of thing did you have in mind?' His voice is low and gruff now and the sound of it sends a shiver of awareness across my skin. My whole body seems to have come alive with lust. Heat coils in my stomach.

I try to squash it down, but it still lingers.

'Er, I don't know... you could go wild swimming there?' I blurt.

'We could go *wild* swimming?' he says with meaning, like it's an innuendo and it suddenly occurs to me what he's suggesting. That the two of us go there and swim naked.

No, no, no. That's a really bad idea.

'I didn't mean—' I say quickly.

But he cuts me off. 'Okay then. Let's go swimming,' he says, starting towards the lake, his pace picking up so I have to take two steps to his one.

'Wait! I didn't mean right now, with me!' I pant, trying to keep up with him.

'Why not? I'm in the mood for moving on today. You've inspired me.'

How can I argue with that?

I can't squash his enthusiasm now.

And I'll be doing it with him as a friend. Purely a friend.

It only takes another minute to get there and as soon as we're standing on the bank, I see him start to undo the button at the top of his jeans.

I have a moment of panic. This is a terrible idea. Especially if I'm now going to have to watch him undress and reveal his amazing body and not be allowed to touch him.

'It's going to be freezing in there,' I point out, perhaps a little late in the day.

'No shit,' he says with a grin.

My heart turns over at the glee in his expression and I see a flash of a younger Jonah before me. The person with all the hope and excitement of his future to come, before it all came crashing down around him and led to so much disappointment and shame.

I watch in stupefied fascination as he steps out of his jeans, revealing his long, muscular legs. My pulse begins to race at the sight and my heart nearly breaks through my chest when he grasps the hem of his t-shirt and whips it over his head. He clearly works out, and I swallow hard as I take in the lean muscles of his arms, then the six pack of his stomach, my gaze finally dropping to the defined V of his hips. Will his boxers be removed next? I wonder wildly.

But it seems that's as unclothed as he's willing to get, because he turns to look at me with an expression of impatient expectation, as if he's wondering what my problem is with stripping to my underwear in front of him in the cool, spring air.

'Come on. What are you waiting for? This was your idea, remember?'

'I know, but I was thinking... maybe do it in the summer months when the water's a bit more temperate?' My voice comes out as a croak.

'Don't be a wimp. Where's your sense of spirit gone?'

I wince at this and remind myself that if Dee was here, she probably would strip off and go swimming with him. She's always been much more adventurous than me and I've often wished I had her daring. Perhaps now's the time to see what that would feel like. To stop being the dull, practical Bea and go wild for a change. It could be fun.

And if Dee would do it, then so should I – just to stay in character, if nothing else.

'Okay,' I say, making up my mind. 'Let's do it. Cold water dips are supposed to be good for you, right?'

'Right. You'll feel totally euphoric afterwards,' he says, with what looks suspiciously like a twinkle in his eye.

'If I don't have a heart attack first,' I mutter.

'You won't,' Jonah assures me.

The way his eyes have lit up with the challenge stokes a wave of pleasure inside me. I'm actually responsible for making him feel just a little bit better about himself right now. It's an uplifting thought.

My mood wobbles though when I realise I'm going to have to take at least some of my clothes off in front of him. There's no way I should get into the water in jeans, so I undo them and slide them down my legs, then step out of them. My t-shirt and my underwear stay firmly on though. Luckily, the hem is long and falls to mid-way down my thighs so my knickers aren't on show.

This is so weird. I can't believe I've just whipped my trousers off in front of my boss like this. But then, he stopped feeling like my boss a while ago. He's just Jonah now. Hot, smart, handsome Jonah.

Ooohhh.

'Okay. You first,' he says, waving me forward, his face a mask of nonchalance.

My heart is thumping against my chest and I feel it reverberate in my throat. I'm actually a little bit scared about just how painful this is going to feel on my poor, delicate, un-acclimatised-to-cold skin.

Tentatively, I dip my foot into the water where it laps gently against the grassy bank. It's very shallow where we're going to enter the lake so it'll take a while to wade out far enough to swim. If we get that far.

A shiver runs from my toes all the way up my leg and goose-bumps prickle across my skin.

A low chuckle behind me makes me turn around and I see Jonah is watching me, his arms folded across his broad, bare chest and an amused grin playing on his lips.

I try not to fixate on the way his biceps bulge in a very distracting manner. He's really broad across the shoulders and they too are well muscled. In all, he's an exceptionally fine spec-imen of a human being.

Dragging my eyes away from him, I turn and face the lake again, digging my fingernails into my palms before lowering my foot fully into the water. I try not to squeal as it immediately turns into a block of ice.

'You're really going to do it, aren't you?' Jonah says with disbe-lief in his voice.

I have to, now he's said that. I can't chicken out now. Dee wouldn't.

'Yup. And so are you. That's the deal.'

I put my other foot in, then bite my lip as I start to wade deeper into the water. I have no idea how I'm going to get to the point where I can bear to get to chest height, based on how numb my feet are already. This is torture.

I'm up to just below my knees when there's the sound of splashing water behind me and a second later, I feel big drops of it hit the backs of my legs. This time, I do squeal and I spin around to see that Jonah has followed me into the lake, but is still right next to the bank. It seems he thinks it's funny to splash me from this position and I cross my arms and glare at him.

'Hey! No splashing!' I shout.

He just laughs. The sound of it echoes around the lake. I can't help but grin. It's wonderful to see his face so alive with pleasure. Since the moment I met him, I've mostly seen him scowl. It's amazing how much younger he looks now the grumpiness has lifted. And how much hotter.

Oh my goodness, I really need to get a grip.

Before I can start wading back to where he's standing, he dips down and scoops up another handful of water.

'Don't you dare!' I warn him, picking up my pace in an attempt to reach him before he has a chance to spray my front with icy droplets as well.

But I'm not fast enough.

He flings the water at me, splashing me all down my front. The water soaks into my t-shirt and I let out an 'eek!'.

Giving a bark of laughter, he bends down, poised to do it again.

But I'm not having that. He doesn't get to stay dry whilst soaking me with freezing lake water. So I bend down too, forming my hands into a scoop, then dipping them just below the surface. When they're full of water, I fling it towards him, catching him right in the face and across the top of his bare shoulders.

He lets out his own surprised yelp at the shock of the cold against his skin, standing up and wiping the droplets from his chin, before turning a playful hard stare on me.

'You're going to regret that,' he taunts me, but the teasing tone in his voice excites me rather than scares me. What's he going to do? Try and dunk me into the water?

I'm ready for him if he does try that.

My competitive nature is back with a vengeance.

I take a defensive stance, crouching down with my feet

planted wide and my hands in front of me, palms forward, fingers pointing down, ready to either deflect any advance he makes or to dip and scoop another handful of water to fling at him. My heart is racing with adrenaline, but it's giving me a lovely, heady sort of feeling of joy. I've not played with someone like this since I was a kid. Since before my parents split up.

I realise I'm actually having fun. I've had to be the sensible one for so long, I've forgotten what that feels like.

And it feels wonderful.

Jonah narrows his eyes when he sees the determination on my face and mirrors my action.

It's a stand-off. Who's going to move first?

I jerk forwards in a feint, as if I'm going for the scoop-and-fling, but pull myself back at the last moment. He flinches in response, as if convinced I'm going straight for the offensive move, but when he realises I'm only teasing, he raises his eyebrows in challenge.

'Hmm, you have spirit, young one. Prepare for battle,' he goads me.

I laugh at the expression on his face. Now he's dropped the grumpy act around me, his whole demeanour has taken on a much friendlier, more playful vibe. In fact, he seems like a completely different person. One I like even more, if that's possible.

My body rushes with a tingly sort of excitement, which I try to squash. I'm only setting myself up for disappointment here. This thing between us is off limits to me.

A sinking feeling of shame returns. I think we've done a really stupid thing here, Dee and I. He's never going to believe that the Dee that comes back is the same woman he's spent the last week with. She acts so differently from me. I never should have stayed for the extra day. I was tempting fate. Why did I do it? Why?

I know why.

Of course I do.

I couldn't bear to abandon him.

Because I've fallen for him.

'Hey. Are you okay? I was only kidding around,' Jonah says, and I realise I've been staring at him, probably with a deep frown on my face as my anxious thoughts raced away from me.

I don't know what to say any more, so tear my gaze away, scoop up a big handful of water and throw it at him.

He takes it full in the face again and, clearly thinking I was only pretending to be stricken, he swats it out of his eyes before retaliating by using the flat of his hand to repeatedly fling big globs of water right back at me.

I hold up my hands in front of my face to deflect it and when it finally stops, I realise he's moved closer to me, so that we're standing only a couple of feet apart now.

He's grinning at me, like he thinks he's won.

Which he kind of has. He's totally won me.

I want to cry. What a mess this situation is. How can I have fallen for the one person I'm not able to have?

'Thanks, Dee. I'm starting to feel an awful lot better about being in this place now,' he says, closing the gap between us so he can reach forward and push my sodden hair away from where it's sticking to my face. 'I don't think I've enjoyed myself so much in years.'

There's a strange, soft look in his eyes now as he gazes at me. He's such a handsome man and there's so much character in his face, I feel like I could look at it for ever and not get bored.

I can't look away; I'm trapped by my attraction to him. It's like a magnet pulling me in.

Heat radiates from his naked torso towards me and I shiver a little, but not with cold. With nerves. Because this feels like a significant moment. It's make or break. Whatever happens next will change my life in a way I'm not prepared for.

He moves infinitesimally closer to me and my entire body rushes with an electric sort of need.

'I have to tell you something,' he says.

Oh God. I can feel the weight of what I think is coming bearing down on me.

The way he's looking at me is giving me chills. Good chills, but also scary ones. Because I know he's about to say something he really shouldn't. I can't let him. It wouldn't be fair.

'I think I'm falling for you.'

No.

No.

It's the one thing I've been wanting to hear coming from his mouth since the first moment I saw him. But not like this. Not when he thinks I'm my sister.

I want to cry.

How did I let this happen? What an idiot I've been. Because I've fallen for him too, of course. Deeply. Totally.

But I can't do this to him. How could I ever explain it without sounding like a crazy person? I'm a fraud. This whole situation is a lie. But I can never tell him that because it might destroy him all over again and I can't bear the thought of being the person that does that to him.

'I'm not...'

'Not what? Not into this?'

'No. That's not what I—'

'Then what?'

'I don't know how to—'

'Is it because you're working for me? That I'm technically

your boss? Because we can fix that. I'll step away from the running of the hotel and get Cara to manage things and I'll concentrate on the cider making. It's what I'm most interested in doing anyway. Or if you wanted, you could run it with me, as a partner. We could look into getting a business loan together—'

'No!' I blurt, feeling all sense of control slipping away from me.

'No, it's not about that? Or no, you don't want me to make cider for a living?'

'Neither.'

'Then what? What's the problem? I feel like we have something good going on here. Did I imagine it?'

'No. You didn't imagine it.'

'I knew it.'

But he doesn't move; he's waiting for me to make the first move this time.

But I can't. I shouldn't. I mustn't.

But I do.

Some devilish instinct takes me over and I step forwards and press my mouth to his, sliding my hands into his hair and feeling our bodies meet, skin to damp skin.

And it's so good. So right.

The feel of his mouth on mine is exquisite.

His lips part and instinctively, I slide my tongue against his, loving the taste of him.

Through my fog of lust, I'm aware of his hands gripping my hips and the press of his erection against my stomach.

Ohhh. I want more, so much more.

But I can't have it.

It's not mine to have.

This is everything I shouldn't want right now.

But I do want it. So much I ache.

A sob works its way up from my chest, but I manage to suppress it at the last second before he can hear my distress. The effort of doing this brings me to my senses.

I have to stop this. And I have to tell him why.

'Wait, Jonah, wait—' I mutter against his mouth.

Reluctantly, he draws away from me. I can feel his entire body trembling with the effort to stop this going further. Just as mine is.

'That was all you this time. You kissed me first,' he points out, his breath coming quickly.

'I know. It's not... it's just... I have to tell you something.'

I can't believe I have to say this.

I screw my eyes shut.

'I'm not Dee,' I whisper.

Tentatively, I open my eyes and see complete confusion in his.

There's a heavy silence while he tries to process what I've just said. His gaze roves my face, his brow pinched, as if he's looking for the joke, waiting for the punchline.

'What? What do you mean?' He's utterly baffled, understandably.

'My name's Beatrice. Bea. I'm Dee's twin sister.' I swallow, my throat dry with fear.

'Sister,' he says, but it's not a question, it's a statement of fact. Cold and to the point. Like he's just put two and two together and all the inconsistencies he's noticed without consciously realising are suddenly making sense to him.

'Yes. We're twins.'

'You said that already. Identical, I'm guessing.' Again, it's not a question.

'Yes.' My heart is thumping so hard, it feels as though it might break out of my chest.

'What the hell is going on? Why are you here and not Dee? What the—? This is surreal!'

'I know, I'm sorry, I can explain. I'm, er, I was taking over for Dee for a few days because she hurt her ankle and couldn't walk.'

'What the fuck? Are you serious?'

He takes a couple of strides away from me, as if repelled by my words.

'I know. I get that it must sound completely crazy. But she was terrified you'd fire her if she wasn't able to do her job so I said I'd step in and help.'

'By impersonating your sister.'

I swallow again. My throat feels like it's been rubbed with sandpaper and I'm painfully aware of hot, panicky tears beginning to form in my eyes.

He's angry. So angry, he's trembling. His eyes are dark and full of distaste. Something I've not encountered before, from anyone.

It's actually quite horrifying.

Icy dread sinks through me and my stomach rolls. Where has the playful, jokey Jonah gone?

'I was just trying to help,' I repeat weakly.

'You lied to me.' He folds his arms across his chest, his shoulders so tense now, I can see the cords of muscles moving under his skin.

'Not deliberately. At least... I guess, yes. Okay, I did lie. But to help my sister out. Not to hurt you in any way.'

'Yeah, well, you did hurt me. How am I supposed to believe anything you say now? You betrayed my trust. I told you things about me... really personal things. And all the time, you were pretending to be someone you're not.'

'I wasn't. I've always been me. Just not the me you thought I was.' It sounds completely lame when I say it, but I don't care. I can't bear the thought of him being angry with me.

'That makes absolutely no sense and you know it.'

'I'm sorry. I never meant for any of this to happen.'

'Really? Because it all sounds very well planned to me.'

'No. It wasn't like that. I promise you. I was trying to help.'

'Trying to help yourself. Trying to get close to me and use me for all you could get. You and your bloody incompetent sister. Well, that's the end of it. You're fired.' He shakes his head. 'Dee's fired and you're trespassing. I want you off my property immediately and I never want to see you here again.'

'Jonah, no. Please. Wait!'

But it's no use. He's already striding purposefully away from me, his back ramrod straight and his hands bunched into fists.

I stare after him, at a total loss about what to do. How can I possibly salvage this now? Not only have I hurt Jonah but I've also got Dee fired from the job she's desperate to keep.

All because I couldn't keep my feelings for Jonah in check.

What have I done?

14

JONAH

It's been one long night, then one long day of hell.

I tip the last dregs of whisky from the bottle into my tumbler and knock it back, no longer feeling the burn of the alcohol.

What the hell was I thinking? Allowing myself to get tangled up in feelings for another woman when it went so badly the last time I let myself go there.

Fucking idiot.

Inevitably, I seem to be right back where I started after Tessa left, only this time it feels different. Worse.

I really fell for her. Hard.

I'd thought I was in love with Tessa, but this thing with Dee – no, *Bea*, for fuck's sake – has shown me that was nothing compared to how I feel now.

Wrecked.

Humiliated.

Sad.

Despite feeling all kinds of anger towards her, I still want her. I can't stop thinking about her. I want to see her and talk to her. But I know that would be a terrible idea.

I can't trust her.

I need answers though to calm the swirling thoughts in my head so I can sleep again. And the only other person who can help me with that is the real Dee. Delilah.

Perhaps I should go and confront her about this whole sorry mess, since it sounds like she was just as much to blame for making such a fucking fool out of me.

And I'll get the satisfaction of telling her that she's fired to her face.

Yes, that's what I'll do.

I won't go in; I'll just do it on the doorstep. Cold and clean.

I stand up, my head swimming a little from the effect of all the alcohol I've consumed, though I don't feel drunk any more. I'm suddenly clear headed. Purposeful. Affirmative action will help and I can feel my blood pumping through my veins at the thought of getting some sort of closure here.

I head over to my office in the main house and look up Dee's address from the CV she gave me and which I never read properly. If I had, would I have been fooled by this crazy sister swap thing they had going?

I scan down it, distracted for a moment as I look for clues. I'm not sure what I'm searching for, but somewhere in the back of my mind, I'm aware I'm trying to find something to make me feel better about being taken for such a ride.

The CV's actually a bit of a mess, with a lot of inconsistencies. There's a strange mix of her having a Business degree but also arts-based work experience and outside interests. Now I look at it, I can pick out the mixture of the two sisters – one using the other's qualifications to land the job in the first place, I suspect.

Well, that's probably fraud or something right there. I'm not entirely sure, but it's definitely dodgy. Dee's been lying about her suitability for the job. A solid case of gross misconduct, so she'll not be able to come back at me for unfair dismissal.

I look at the personal details section. There it is. Her address: a flat in Bath. Sliding my phone out of my pocket, I book a taxi on the app and go outside to wait for it to turn up, pacing back and forth until it does, feeling a renewed sense of purpose as I count down the minutes till I can confront the perpetrator of my latest humiliation.

* * *

The taxi pulls up to a row of Georgian terraced houses and I thank the driver and get out, feeling a bit more sober now.

I've spent the whole journey trying and failing to stop myself from playing out what happened with Bea at the lake yesterday over and over in my head and I feel like I'm going nuts with it.

The way she kissed me. It blew my mind.

I wanted it to happen so much and when it did, my body went into overdrive.

There's a heaviness in my chest now though, weighing me down. A deep, grinding sadness making my head throb.

To go from elation to shocked disbelief was a sucker punch to the gut and I'm still reeling from it.

How could I have not seen it? The total change in attitude and competence should have been a huge red flag, but I was so attracted to the 'new' her, I let it blind me.

And how could she have told those lies right to my face? Mostly lies of omission, sure, but they were still dishonest. I remember with a sting of humiliation how she let me tell her all those personal things about myself. Not just about Tessa, but how I felt about my relationship with my dad.

Shit! I can't believe I told Bea so much about that.

But I thought, at the time, that she cared. Cared about me.

Taking a breath, I walk up to the front door of the town house where Dee's flat is and look for the panel of buzzers.

I need to stay calm now. Be assertive. Do what needs to be done, get some closure and then go home and start all over again.

The mere thought of that makes my heart sink.

I'd got so excited about the idea of developing the hotel with Bea, but that's never going to happen now. I can't be around someone I can't trust.

Her face flashes into my mind and all the air leaves my lungs, as if someone's just elbowed me in the ribs.

I get now why Bea stopped me kissing her after we performed together – the memory of that night now takes on a very different significance in my mind – but why did she then kiss me at the lake? And why go to the trouble of going with me to the rival boutique hotel? What did she have to gain from that?

My thoughts are a mess.

The paranoia is back in full force and I jab angrily at the buzzer for her top floor flat.

The thing is, it doesn't matter now. I don't care any more.

I'm done with her and her games.

Her and her bloody sister.

The door buzzes and clicks open and I step inside and quickly climb all the stairs to the real Dee's flat, taking them two at a time. Now I'm here, I just want to get this over with.

It's right at the top though and I'm out of breath by the time I get there so I take a moment before knocking on the door, waiting for my heart rate to slow so I don't just pant at her when she opens up.

Steeling myself, I raise my fist and bang three times, feeling the flimsy wood shake under my knuckles.

Then I wait impatiently for her to come to the door, my foot tapping a rhythm on the worn carpet.

I have a sudden moment of panic. What am I actually going to say to her? She already knows she's fired, I'm sure. Bea must have told her by now. But I need to stay completely professional about this. I can't give her any reason to come back at me legally.

Perhaps I shouldn't be doing this after drinking.

But it's too late; the door is already swinging open.

I stare at the woman standing in front of me. Her eyes are wide with surprise, as if she's totally floored to see me. She's clearly not brushed her hair today because it's sticking up in messy waves around her head. There's no make-up on her face either and there are dark rings under her eyes, as if she's not slept.

Her brows knit together and she opens her mouth, then closes it again, seemingly lost for words.

I just stand there and gaze at her. Despite her dishevelled state – or perhaps because of it – she's never looked more beautiful and the whole of my insides seem to heat with a fiery need that I've become accustomed to feeling whenever I'm around her.

Her familiar sweet scent hits my senses and instinctively, I draw it in through my nose, pulling it down deep into my lungs.

'Hi Bea,' I say. Because I know without a doubt – without a single ounce of uncertainty – that this isn't Delilah. There's something deep down in my bones that tells me that. The chemistry between us is totally different.

I've always been aware that Dee's attractive, but I never felt the way I did when I was around Bea. Something in me just knew they were different people.

I guess I've been aware of that in the back of my mind, but I've not wanted to fully admit it to myself.

And that my life changed course the day Bea walked into it.

'Hi,' she says, in a rough-sounding voice, as if she's been crying all night.

Has she?

I push away the thump of concern. It shouldn't matter to me whether she's upset or not. It's not my problem.

'I came to see Delilah,' I say, keeping my voice as unemotional as I can in the face of this setback.

'She's not here. We swapped apartments because of her ankle.'

'I see.'

We just stare at each other for a moment, the unspoken angst reverberating in the air between us.

'Do you want to come in?' she asks.

The hope in her eyes nearly breaks me.

But I can't let it.

She made a fool out of me and I shouldn't trust another word she says.

She's bad news.

Really bad.

But despite all this, I can't bring myself to leave.

'Okay,' I say, and as she backs away from the door, I step into the flat and follow her inside.

15

BEATRICE

My legs are shaking as I walk through Dee's hallway and into her living room, intensely aware of Jonah following me.

It's so good to see him. I can hardly believe he's here.

I wish I wasn't in such a state though. I barely slept all night and I was so exhausted and miserable this morning, I ended up bawling for twenty solid minutes in the shower.

My face is now a puffball and my eyes look hollow.

In short, I'm a mess.

'Have you changed your mind about Dee losing her job?' I ask hopefully.

He gives me such a look of angry incredulity, I flinch. 'You've got to be kidding.'

'So you're still angry with me?'

He stares at me for a moment and I swallow uncomfortably in the pause.

'I trusted you with all my shit and the whole time, you were bare-faced lying to me. So yes, I'm still fucking angry with you.'

I hold up both hands in a gesture of acceptance. 'I shouldn't have lied to you. It was wrong of me to do that. I got so carried away with pretending to be Dee, I lost my head. Not that that's an excuse.'

'No, it's not.'

I fold my arms defensively. 'You have every right to be angry. But I promise you, I genuinely meant no harm. I was trying to help.' I inwardly cringe at the pleading in my voice.

His snort is full of disdain. 'Help me with what, exactly? Making me look even more of an idiot? Or did you just fancy stepping into Tessa's vacant place for a bit? See what it was like dating the son of a rock star?'

'That was never my intention. I'm not interested in your dad's fame. Things just... got away from me.'

'Things?'

'How I started to feel about you.'

A frown flickers across his face and he turns away and walks over to the window, his broad back towards me. I can see the tension in his shoulders and my heart turns over.

I can't stand him being so cold with me like this. Not after the closeness we've developed recently. Finally getting him to smile had felt like a massive achievement. I want to see that smile again. Desperately.

'I don't think what I did is on a par with how Tessa treated you.'

He just snorts, still refusing to look at me.

A thread of frustration begins to unravel in my chest. This whole situation is so unfair. I was just trying to help. 'You know what? I think you're using this as an excuse to get out all your residual anger about Tessa and the way she treated you. To find an outlet for the rejection and loss of control you felt. You're still hurting from that, which is totally understandable, but you're taking it out on me and that's not fair.'

He spins around, his face a mask of anger. 'Don't try to psychoanalyse me,' he spits out.

'I'm not. I'm just pointing out the obvious,' I say, determined not to back down. I'm desperate to find a way back to how things were with us and it seems to me the only way to do that is to tackle our issues head on.

He stares up at the ceiling, shaking his head.

I take a tentative step towards him, my hands out in supplication.

'Yes, I messed up, I admit that, but I'm not Tessa. I didn't cheat on you and I didn't walk away from you. In fact, I really wanted to stay, more than anything. I didn't want Dee to come back to her job. I wanted to do it. I still want to do it.'

He looks at me now and I see a flash of something, a break in the fury.

I take another step towards him. We're only a couple of feet apart now. I feel the air between us vibrate with an unspoken passion.

I have to be brave and tell him exactly how I'm feeling or I suspect he's going to walk out of here and I'll never see him again.

'But mostly,' I say, 'I want to be with you. Because I really care about you. In fact... I've... I think... I think we'd be good together. Be good *for* each other.'

He shakes his head again, his eyes hard. 'I don't know about that.'

'What? What don't you know?'

'That we'd be good for each other.'

'Why not? Why wouldn't we be?'

'I'm too broken to have a relationship right now.'

I force back a sob of frustration. 'You're not!'

Again, he shakes his head at me. 'You're right. I am still angry with Tessa. I need to work my way past it before I can trust someone again.'

'Okay. I understand. Well, I can wait for you. I will wait. For as long as it takes.'

'Don't bother. We can't ever work now because I'll never be able to trust you again.'

He starts to move towards the door and I run in front of him, blocking his way.

'That's not true! Please don't go. Please. We can't leave it like this.'

I reach out and curl my fingers around his tensed forearm in a desperate attempt to stop him from walking around me and out of my life.

And I can't bear the thought of that.

I'm expecting him to shrug my hand off, but he doesn't. Instead, he stands there, rooted to the spot, not looking at me, his whole upper torso radiating tension. I can feel the effort he's expending to keep himself emotionally distant from me pouring off him.

Sensing I have a slim window here to persuade him to stay and talk to me some more, I side-step around in front of him till we're face to face again. He's refusing to look at me though.

'Please give me another chance. I swear I'll never lie to you again.'

I see his throat move as he swallows.

I have an intense urge to kiss him, to show him just how much he means to me. I want to give myself to him fully, make myself so vulnerable, he can see a way to trust me again.

Leaning in closer to him, I catch his scent in the air – spicy and masculine – and I breathe it in deeply.

My head throbs.

I want him so badly, my entire body is aching with need.

'Jonah. Please? We can't leave it like this.'

I can see from the frown on his face that he's battling with himself. I think he's feeling the same need I am, but he's not allowing himself to break.

So, I'm going to have to break his will for him.

Putting my hands on each side of his face, I draw him to me, leaning in closer until our lips are almost touching. I feel him resist for a second and I'm about to back away again, not wanting to force him to do anything he really doesn't want to do, when he lets out a low, frustrated-sounding moan from the depths of his throat and closes the small space between us, crushing his mouth against mine.

My heart leaps and I kiss him back hard, loving the feel of his skin beneath my hands, his breath mingling with mine, his tongue as it slides into my mouth in such a possessive way, it makes me gasp.

Oh God.

I press my body hard up against his and delight in the feel of his erection pushing against me.

He wants me as much as I want him.

I'm jubilant.

Despite his anger with me, there's still a part of him that needs this closeness and connection too.

I sink into it, my body responding instinctively to his. My skin is rushing with heat and a fizzing sort of excitement. Something I've never experienced before. Being physically close to Jonah is on a whole other level compared to the way it's been with anyone else.

His hands move down my body and scoop under my bum and before I know it, he's lifting me up against him.

I wrap my legs around his middle to support me and he spins

us around and takes a couple of steps till he has me pressed up against the wall.

He grinds into me, his body pressing hard against mine and kisses me like he's afraid I'll disappear at any moment and this is his last chance to get what he wants.

I welcome it.

This is what I want. What I've wanted since the moment I saw him.

'Fuck! What are you doing to me?' he mutters against my mouth.

'I'm showing you how much I want you,' I murmur back.

He fists his hand into my hair and holds my head still while he kisses me thoroughly, his tongue sliding deep into my mouth. It's as if he's finally releasing all the tension he's been holding onto through this kiss. There's frustration and anger and need in it, as well as pleasure.

I feel exactly the same. Holding myself back from allowing this to happen has been monumentally hard.

I wriggle and push myself against the bulge at the front of his jeans, wanting, needing to get closer.

He groans at the added friction and steps back, releasing me from where he has me pressed against the wall and turns around so he can walk us over to the bed.

When we get there, he drops me onto my back and I keep my legs wrapped around him while he shuffles us up the mattress until my head hits the pillows. He then proceeds to roughly remove every piece of clothing from my body with a frown of concentration on his beautiful face. Then strips his own clothes off too, flinging them away from him as if they offend him.

'Condoms... in the drawer,' I say, pointing to the bedside table.

Without a word, he leans over and yanks the drawer open,

locating a strip of them and tearing one off, then unwrapping it with swift fingers and sheathing himself.

I watch the focused concentration on his face as he does all this, till he looks back at me and our gazes lock. He's still frowning, but there's an intensity in his eyes that's giving me excited chills.

I'm expecting him to say something, but he doesn't. Instead, he slides his fingers between my legs and when he finds how ready I am for him, he kisses me hard on the mouth, then lines up our bodies and slides his cock inside me, inch by delicious inch. Breaking the kiss, he looks into my eyes as he pushes fully into me, his gaze never wavering from mine. After an excruciating few moments of anticipation, he finally draws back and starts to thrust. It's fast and furious sex and it feels like we're locked together in a sort of fight for supremacy.

I give back as good as I'm getting.

We grunt and moan and gasp in wild abandon, our bodies slapping together hard. It's carnal and animalistic and real. So real.

I've never been so turned on.

Feeling a need to take more control, I rock us to the side and he allows me to roll on top of him, our bodies miraculously staying locked together. I ride him hard, rubbing my clit against his pubic bone and I wrap my fingers around the tops of his arms and hold on as I feel myself begin to come.

It's powerful. So powerful, I lose myself in the sheer pulsing joy of it.

This – this is what I've wanted all along.

To feel this way.

I hear Jonah's own moans of pleasure start to build beneath me and I keep riding him, taking delight in the lingering waves of my orgasm as he comes too, his fingers digging into my hips.

I collapse on top of him, my head next to his on the pillow, feeling his chest rise and fall beneath mine, our bodies hot and our skin slick.

'That's what we both needed, right? Closure,' he whispers into my ear, his breath coming in short, hard pants. 'A full stop to the whole damn circus.'

Sitting up, I frown down at him, my brain slow to catch up with what he just said.

When it finally does, I suck in a sharp breath, aware of a hot dread washing over my whole body.

Before I can reply, he grips my hips and lifts me off him, depositing me on the bed next to him, then rolls away and gets up, leaving me staring after him in shock.

What just happened?

'No. That's not what I need at all,' I say, sitting up. 'I want – you. I want a relationship with you.'

He's searching around for his clothes now and after locating them all, pulls on his boxers, then his jeans. 'Not going to happen. We're done now,' he says as he does up the buttons, not making eye contact with me. 'I'm not ready to have another relationship, especially since I only seem to be attracted to women who end up fucking me over and I really don't want that for myself.'

'I won't fuck you over,' I say, hating the shake in my voice.

'Too late. You already have.'

'Please don't be like that.'

He doesn't respond, just pulls his t-shirt over his head.

I've lost him and I feel desperate about it.

'I love you,' I blurt, then wince at how pathetic and needy that sounds.

'Sure you do, Bea.' He finally turns to look at me for one long moment, tears glinting in his eyes. Then he shakes his head. 'Bye.'

Without another word, he strides out of the room, banging the door closed behind him.

I just sit there, staring after him, then wince as I hear the outer door bang as well as he leaves the house.

So that's it then. He's gone. Probably out of my life for ever.

Getting off the bed on shaky legs, I gather up my clothes and pull them on, forcing back the tears that are threatening to break at any second.

I'm feeling everything right now, but mostly anger at myself.

What the hell did I think would happen? That we'd have sex and it would magically make everything okay? Did I really stoop so low as to try and seduce him into forgiving me? What a bloody fool I am.

But I was desperate. I didn't know what else to do to get through to him.

Having sex wasn't it though.

Idiot!

Now I know how amazing it can be with him, I'm never going to be able to forget it. Or experience the joy of it with him again, judging by his reaction to me afterwards.

I want to cry. But I'm not going to. I have to move forwards, one step at a time and look to the day when I don't feel this way any more.

If only I could say I wish I'd never met Jonah Jacobson, but that would just be another lie.

16

JONAH

After leaving Bea, I get a cab back to Gladbrooke and head straight for the lake. The scene of my humiliation.

Both times.

Flopping down onto the hard bank, I stare out across the water, my vision blurring as tears burn in my eyes.

What the fuck just happened?

I know I was still a bit pissed when I turned up to see her, but I don't think that was the reason I gave in to her seduction so easily.

Truth is, I needed to have sex with her to put an end to the constant ache I've been feeling and it completely clouded my judgement. Stupidly, in the back of my mind, I think I believed it would rid me of those feelings. That once we'd banged, I'd get her out of my system.

But no.

I just want her even more now.

It was incredible, the connection I felt with her in those moments. Like the first deep drink of water when you're parched.

But it scared the shit out of me too, which is why I had to get out of there right away. I know it was a fucking cruel way to behave and I'll have really hurt her, but I had to do it. I needed to make it a clean break: something we couldn't come back from. Because otherwise I know I'd be tempted to go back to her and I can't do that. I have to protect myself.

I can't get hurt again and go back to that dark place I was in a few months ago.

Except now I just feel raw and exposed, much more so than I did before because I know how good it can be with her. Why the hell did I let that happen? I've made everything a million times harder for myself. Because I really don't want to care about her.

Ha. Too late, Jacobson.

And she said she loves me. But does she really? Or was she just telling me what she thought I wanted to hear? You see? How can I trust anything she tells me now?

I've learnt my lesson, after Tessa. If I find someone has lied to me, that's it. Finito. No second chances. I'm not getting side-swiped like that again.

I have to be able to trust my partner and that ship's well and truly sailed with Bea.

Time to move on. Even if the thought of it fills me with dread.

Can it only be yesterday that I was excited for the future for the first time in ages?

I suddenly feel so crushingly alone. Bea's gone, my dad's constantly abroad, my mum is in London and too busy to see me most of the time and my brother couldn't give a shit about me.

When I was with Bea, I really thought I was with someone who truly wanted to be around me because she liked me. *Me.* Not because I have a famous father or a cool career that got me invited to all the best parties.

That she was a really genuine person who I could trust.

But it's clear to me now that I really can't.

* * *

Beatrice

Despite desperately hoping he'll change his mind and come
back to the flat, I don't see or hear from Jonah again that day. Or
the next.

Deep down, I know that if he was going to come back, he'd
have done it by now.

So, I guess that's it for us. It's over as quickly as it started.

If only it didn't feel like I've had a hole ripped in my chest
and my heart removed.

I never thought it would be possible to fall in love with
someone so quickly and so deeply, but I was wrong about that.

I wish to goodness I wasn't.

I miss him. And I miss going to Gladbrooke. It had started to
feel like a new life, one I could get excited about. One I wanted to
hold onto and grow into. One I properly belonged in.

It had had real purpose and a clear, foreseeable future.
Something my working life up till that point hadn't had. As
determined as I was to work with Jem and build our fledgling
business, it had always felt a little nebulous. As if we were
playing at being adults and business owners – not that we could
even call ourselves that yet with the company in its infancy.

Needing to distract myself from thinking about Jonah, I have a
quick shower, get dressed in my business clothes and go over to my
flat-cum-office, glad of the change of scene. Once there, I make
myself a strong coffee and open up my email, only to find a mail
telling me Jem and I have been rejected for our funding application.

So that's the end of that too.

In some ways, it's a relief because I've had a nagging feeling recently that it wasn't what I really wanted to do; I was just too afraid to admit it. Not just to Jem, but to my dad. Mostly to my dad, if I'm honest. I know he's going to be really disappointed when I tell him the business is already dead in the water.

He's always had such high hopes for me and I'm going to let him down.

Though, honestly, surprisingly, I find I don't care about that as much as I care that I'll never see Jonah again.

It had really felt like we connected, on such a deep, organic level.

That we're meant to be together.

The whole of my being hurts at the thought that that can never happen now. I well and truly messed it up by trying to live Dee's life for her.

Or maybe for me?

Huh. Yes, I think that might be it. I wanted a new direction, so I tried to steal hers.

I should have listened to Jem. He was right. I never should have got involved in this crazy plan of Dee's.

But then I never would have met Jonah.

And I don't regret the time I spent with him, not one bit, despite how I'm feeling now.

Better to have loved and lost, and all that.

Isn't it?

I put my head in my hands and stare down at my keyboard.

What now though? For the first time in my life, I find myself with no idea about the next steps to take.

* * *

Jonah

It's been nearly a week now, since I last saw Bea, and the heavy ache in my chest still hasn't gone away.

I've been walking around the hotel in a complete daze, not really engaging with anything going on around me. Luckily, we're quiet for bookings at the moment and Cara's taken up the slack, stepping in for me after I told her I had some personal issues to deal with.

I know she's probably guessed it's to do with Dee, but I haven't admitted to being duped by the ridiculous sister swap for fear of looking like a complete chump.

I'm probably projecting, but it seems like the whole atmosphere of the hotel has changed since Bea left though. It feels silent and devoid of warmth now. She really brought the place to life while she was here. And me too, of course.

Her passion and positivity inspired something in me, which now seems to be sadly lacking again.

I've lost my purpose, I guess.

I want it back.

And I want the excitement and momentum we got going for the project to return. But I can't figure out a way to do that without her.

It's funny, but it's made me realise I was crazy to imagine things would ever have worked out here with Tessa. She was never going to be happy living and working at Gladbrooke, so far out of London and away from the celebrity scene she's become so attached to.

And strangely, I find now that I really don't care that she left. It was for the best.

One good thing about meeting Bea is that it's made me recognise how little I actually liked spending time with Tessa when I was sober. It was all about the partying with her.

And thinking about her now, I realise I'm feeling... nothing.

She was never the right woman for me. I just imagined she fitted the rock-star persona I thought I wanted.

Whereas whenever I think about Bea, I get a weird heavy ache in my chest. Like part of me is missing.

I should probably just hand the place back to my dad for him to sell right away. I don't want to run the place on my own.

And more to the point, I don't want to do it without Bea.

17

BEATRICE

It's been a painful, lonely week, with no contact from Jonah and still no sign of Dee and Jem. From the messages she's been sending me, it sounds like the storm's wreaked havoc in that part of Europe and a lot of people have been trapped and grounded whilst waiting for it to blow over and for safe travel to resume again.

I pretended to her that I'd gone through with the 'twisting my ankle' plan so she didn't have to worry about that while she was clearly really stressed about the situation on the island. I feel bad about not telling her right away about being fired, but I figured there wasn't anything she could do about it and the last thing she needed was more bad news. Jonah clearly hasn't been directly in touch with her either, so at least that's a blessing.

I can't imagine what state they'll all be in when they finally make it home though.

It sounds like it's been a real ordeal.

Just as I'm thinking this, there's the sound of the door opening to the flat and I hear voices as Dee and Jem come inside and head towards the kitchen.

I feel a surge of relief that they're back. At least I'll have some friendly faces around me now after carrying around the memory of the hard look on Jonah's face just before he walked out on me.

But when I hurry out of the office and find them having what appears to be a whispered conversation in the kitchen, neither of them has particularly happy expressions on their faces.

Uh oh.

'Hey, you're back,' I say stupidly.

Dee comes straight over to hug me and I sink into her arms, feeling a sudden overwhelming need to cry. But I hold it back, steeling myself against it. I don't want the first thing they have to do, after stepping in through the door, is mollify me.

'So, you finally escaped from the storm,' I say into her hair.

'Only just,' she replies, but there's a heaviness to her voice that shoots worry through me.

'Is everything okay?' I ask, pulling back to look her in the face.

There's a moment where I think I see a flash of sadness in her eyes, but she quickly covers it with a smile. 'All good. Just glad to be home safe. The journey back was mostly smooth,' she says. Again, there's a hint of darkness in her voice and I wonder for a wild second whether there's some subtext there meant for Jem to hear.

'So, are you two still speaking to each other?' I joke, wanting to test out this theory.

There's a slightly awkward pause before they both say, 'Yes.'

Liars.

There's definitely something going on here that the two of them don't want me to know about.

'How about you?' Dee asks quickly before I can say anything more. 'How did the festival go?'

'Oh. Great. It went really well.' I force back a wave of sadness as I remember how much fun I'd had organising and running it. I'm feeling almost nostalgic about it now, even though it only ended a few days ago.

Having sex with Jonah seems to have turned my world upside down and inside out and it's making everything else feel very distant.

'You don't look very happy about it,' Dee points out, her eyebrows knitted.

I try to smile and brush away her worry, but to my horror, my eyes fill with tears.

I'm going to have to tell her everything and I don't even know where to start.

'I... er... I've got some bad news, I'm afraid,' I say in a shaky voice.

Her frown deepens. 'Are you okay? What's going on?' She looks panicked now.

I sense Jem shift next to me, but I can't look him in the face. He's got some bad news of his own coming, but I can't get into that right now.

'I made a real mess of things, Dee. I'm so sorry.'

'What do you mean?' She moves closer to me, her head cocked to one side.

'I... I had to tell Jonah I was pretending to be you and... he fired me. Well, you. He fired you.'

She stares at me for a moment, clearly trying to unpick what I've just told her.

'Right. Okay. And why did you have to tell him?'

This, of course, was the trickiest bit to explain.

'Um.' I clear my throat. 'We, er. We started to get close.'

Dee widens her eyes. 'When you say close...?'

'We kissed.' I screw up my eyes, not able to look at her now.

When I finally open them and peek at her, her expression shows a mixture of surprise and delight.

Weird.

'And he kissed you back?' she asks.

'Yes.'

'Wow. So, you two are a thing now?'

I shake my head. 'No. We ended up sleeping together, but he's really angry with me for lying to him about who I really am. I think it's over now.'

Jem makes a strange noise in the back of his throat. Apparently, he's uncomfortable listening in on us talking about our sex lives – or lack of them in my case, because he mutters, 'I'm just going to check on my email in the office,' then strides out of the room before we can say anything.

Dee is staring at me like she can't quite process what she's hearing.

To my frustration, a tear pools in the corner of my eye, then slides down my cheek.

'Oh, Bea! You poor, poor thing,' Dee says, breaking out of her trance and wrapping her arms around me again. 'Don't cry. At least, don't cry about me losing my job. I don't care about that. I'll get another one. I was never any good at it anyway and I was fooling myself it would all magically work out and help turn me into some famous artist. What was I thinking! Clearly, Jonah wasn't interested in a relationship with me either. He wouldn't kiss *me* back.' She attempts a smile but I can see in her eyes that she's hurting. Badly.

'I don't know how it happened,' I say in a begging voice. 'I never meant it to, I swear.'

'Yeah, well. Sometimes these things creep up on us and take us out at the knees.'

I give her a grim frown. 'I never believed in love at first sight before. And then I met Jonah.'

'So you love him?' she asks me in a gentle voice.

'It sounds crazy, I know. I've only just met him, but there's something about him... I just know, deep in my bones, that he's the man for me. It's an instinct, not something I can explain.'

'That's love for you,' Dee agrees.

'I can't believe this situation. It's so messed up!' Another tear escapes from my eye and I brush it away angrily.

'Are you sure there's nothing to be done here?'

'Yes. I'm sure. You should have seen the way he looked at me when he left. He doesn't trust me any more. He can't. Not after I lied to him the way I did.'

'Because I made you.'

'You didn't make me. I chose to do it. I could have said no.'

'Hmm. I'm not sure about that. I basically emotionally black-mailed you into doing it.'

I bat away her words. 'Well, it doesn't matter any more. It's done and can't be undone. We're both just going to have to move on with our lives in different directions.' I take a breath. 'Speaking of which, I need to let Jem know something. I'll be back in a moment and we'll talk some more and see if we can work out what we're going to do about getting you a new job.'

She opens her mouth to reply, but I don't give her the chance to speak before walking out of the kitchen and into the office.

Jem is sitting at his desk, staring at an email which is up on his computer screen.

He turns to look at me with a strange expression on his face. It's as if he knows what I'm about to tell him.

'We didn't get the funding,' I say, wanting to get it over with quickly. 'So it looks like this business isn't going to work out the way we'd hoped, barring any miracles.'

He just nods once, but surprisingly doesn't look either shocked or devastated. 'Yeah, well, maybe it's for the best.' He leans back in his chair and rubs his hand over his face. I see now that he looks exhausted.

'Really? How so?'

'I've been wondering whether this type of software is where we want to put all our effort. Especially with the rise of AI.'

'Oh.'

'And.' He pauses, then looks me right in the eye. 'I've been offered a job, which I'm seriously considering taking.'

'Oh,' I say again, only this time with a sting of hurt. He's really giving up on running a business with me that easily? But then I know he needs money to pay for his mum's care and it doesn't look as if he's going to be making much, if any, of that if we're going to have to start all over again.

'Sorry, Bea. It's a great opportunity, but it'll be intensive and won't leave me any time outside of it to work on something new with you.'

There's a small cough behind me and I turn to see that Dee's come into the room.

Jem darts a glance at her, then looks back at me. 'It's based in London. I'll be working for the guy your dad introduced me to this week. The one who owns the island we were just staying on.'

'I see.' This feels like another blow, though at the same time I'm really pleased for Jem. He's a brilliant, incredibly kind man and deserves to be successful. 'Okay. Well, far be it for me to stand in your way. I want you to be happy and if this is the way to make that happen then you have my every blessing.'

'I'm really sorry, Bea. I wanted to make this business work with you, but it looks like it's not meant to happen.'

I nod stiffly. 'Yeah. We should cut our losses. And you should definitely take that job, if it's something you want to do.'

He looks down at his keyboard and nods. 'I think it is.'

I feel the air move behind me as Dee shifts on the spot. 'So, you're going to take it?' she asks. Her voice sounds clipped and I spin around to see she has a pained expression on her face.

'Yeah,' is all Jem says.

There's a strange tension in the air now, but I can't quite put my finger on why.

'What's going on with you two?' I ask, looking between them both.

'Nothing,' Jem says, getting up from his chair. 'I'm going to head home. I have things to arrange,' he says, squeezing my shoulder as he passes me and walks past Dee, who's hovering by the door.

Neither of them say another word to the other.

As soon as he's gone and we hear the sound of the door clicking back into place, Dee gives me a tight smile.

'Okay. I'm going to go and see Jonah and sort this mess out.'

For a second, I wonder whether I've heard her correctly.

'What?'

'I'm going over there now to explain the whole thing to him and tell him he's an idiot to walk away from you.' She swivels on the spot and starts to walk towards the door.

After a stunned second, I hurry after her.

'Wait, Dee. Don't go. He's not going to change his mind.'

'You don't know that. And anyway, it's me he's really angry with. If I deflect his annoyance from you towards me, maybe he'll have the good grace to see what's really at stake here and come to his senses. I suspect he already knows he's made a mistake, because he's not stupid. He's hurt and he's put up a protective wall around himself and he just needs someone to make a chink in it and let in the light – point out the obvious. That he'd be crazy to give you up.'

'But—'

'I'm going to look after you for a change. You've been such a good sister to me and I've taken advantage of that too many times. You give so much to other people, especially your family, and it's not fair that you don't get to have what you deserve. It's time you started putting yourself first and you should tell Dad to sod off if he doesn't agree with the way you want to live your life. He's too bloody controlling, always has been. Let's be real here: we're never going to live up to his expectations so why even try? That way madness lies. Jem will be totally fine too. You should do *you* for once.' She puts her hands on my shoulders and looks me directly in the eye. 'You're not my mother and I don't need you to be – not that I don't appreciate everything you've done for me – but it's time I sorted my own life out now. And I'm going to help you sort yours in any way I can.'

'What are you—?'

'Wait here. I'm going to fix this,' she says. And before I can say another word, she's out of the door and getting into her car, then pulling quickly away from the kerb with a screech of tyres.

I stare after her, my mouth hanging open, wondering what the hell's got into my sister.

18

JONAH

I'm in my office, totally failing to look at anything work related, or to pick up the phone to my dad and tell him I've decided to quit the hospitality business, when I hear the sound of a car driving fast up the driveway, then coming to a screeching halt in the car park.

Going to the window, I look out to see Bea's car has just pulled into a parking space at an untidy angle.

So maybe it's not Bea.

Maybe it's Dee?

My stomach flips at the thought of seeing either of them right now, but especially Bea. I'd told myself not to think about her any more – not that I seemed to be able to remotely manage that because everything I look at here reminds me of her – and the last thing I need is her, or her evil twin, turning up and wrecking my head again.

The car door swings open and a woman with a blonde bob gets out.

It could still be either of them.

Until she starts to walk towards the staff entrance to the hotel and I know in an instant which sister it is.

Dee.

As I watch her stride purposefully closer to me, I find myself amused by the realisation that I can tell the two of them apart instantly, despite them being identical.

There's just something missing as I gaze at my ex-employee. The real one. No lurch in my chest. No quickening of my pulse. Nada.

Leaving the office, I walk into the corridor to meet her as she bangs in through the door.

She comes to an abrupt halt in front of me, her face set in a scowl of displeasure.

'Hello, Dee. Did your sister not tell you you're fired?' I state, folding my arms.

She blinks at me slowly. 'Yes, I did get that memo. And I've come to tell you that that's fair enough, I deserve it, but Bea doesn't deserve the treatment she's getting.'

I let out a snort, taken aback by this verbal attack. 'How so?'

Dee lets out a deep sigh. 'Can we go for a walk in the grounds or something? I don't want to do this in the corridor.'

I shrug. 'It doesn't matter to me where we do this. You're still fired.'

'Noted,' she says dryly, swivelling on the spot, then walking back out of the hotel.

I stand there for a moment, considering whether I should actually follow her or go back to my office, just to show her who's calling the shots, but something in me wants to hear what she's got to say. I'm intrigued to see what her next play is. Is she here to try and get her job back? Or something else?

Pushing away a strange surge of hope, I take a breath then follow her outside.

She's waiting impatiently for me, scuffing her toe against the gravel of the car park, but when she sees me emerge, she starts walking again towards the gardens in front of the house.

I catch her up and we walk in silence for a few beats, before she finally draws in an audible breath and says, 'Look, she only did this because I begged her to.'

When I glance at her, her face is a picture of remorse – something I never thought I'd see.

'Seriously, Jonah. It's not her fault. The mere thought of hurting you, of hurting anyone, gives her the horrors, I can promise you that. She's beating herself up badly for how this all turned out. She is and always has been the kindest, sweetest, most giving, caring person I've ever met. And I know I'm bound to say that because she's my sister, but she's also been my nemesis all my life because she's always done everything perfectly. Up until now, anyway. She's never been in trouble for anything in her life because she can't allow herself to make mistakes. It's because of our dad. He's such a tough person to please but she's somehow managed to do it. Which is no mean feat, believe me. I've been trying all my life too, but I still haven't managed it. Not once. But Bea, she's something else – so resilient in the face of everything going completely tits up. She always knows what to do to fix things. Problem is, it means she puts everyone else and their wants before herself. Particularly me. She even cut off her beautiful hair to help me out. That's love.'

'And what's this got to do with me?' I ask, though I feel a sting of shame at how cold that sounds. But I've got to protect myself. I'm not being humiliated and lied to again.

'For God's sake, Jonah, you don't know how lucky you are to have her in your life. She's the most loyal person you could ever hope to meet. And she loves you. *Really* loves you. I've never seen her like this before. She's absolutely bereft. For someone who puts being successful at work above all else, she absolutely couldn't give a shit about it right now. All she can think about is you and how much she's hurt you and how she can't fix it. It's driving her crazy, I can tell.'

'Not my problem,' I re-iterate. 'I've got my own shit to deal with.' But there's less conviction in my voice now. For some reason, my heart's started pounding hard.

Dee lets out a loud, frustrated sigh. 'Get over yourself, will you? So you've had some bad luck and humiliation in the past. So what? We all have. It's how you move on from it that counts.'

She comes to an abrupt halt and I stop too. We turn to face each other.

'Okay, so she made a mistake,' Dee says, holding up both hands. 'It turns out she's not as perfect as we all thought. Which is actually a relief to me. And sure, it wasn't a great thing to do to you, but she accepts that and she's sorry and wants to fix it. She's not leaving you, Jonah; she's in for the long haul. Anyway, I just thought you needed to hear the truth. The whole truth. It's up to you, of course, but take it from me: you'll rue the day you turned down my sister's love if you decide not to see her again. She's one in a million.'

And with that, she turns on her heel and walks away from me.

I watch her go, my head buzzing with thoughts.

She's right of course. It'd be madness to let my fear of being made a fool of again stop me from having a relationship with Bea now. I know, deep down, that she's truly sorry for how things turned out and that she never meant to hurt me.

It's not fair for me to keep punishing her. Especially, as she pointed out, I also seem to be intent on punishing her for what happened with Tessa too.

But then, I wasn't exactly thinking straight about anything at that point.

I'm thinking straight now though.

I want Bea back. Very, very badly. And not just as an employee, but as my partner.

Because I've fallen in love with her.

She's all I can think about. The way she moves, the way she smells, the beautiful curve of her smile and the warmth of her body when it was pressed to mine. We fit so perfectly. Even if it was an impulsive, inelegant coupling. A heat-of-the-moment thing.

So fucking hot.

But there was tenderness beneath the desire too.

I still feel it now.

I want her back in my life.

I've been so afraid to put my trust in someone again, it's blinded me to what I actually need. It's Bea. She's my perfect fit. And, despite what I said to her, I do understand now why she went along with the stupid ruse she and Dee cooked up between them. She did it because she cares deeply about her sister and that's something I can't ignore. I want that too, to be in her circle of warmth and love and protection.

Even though it hurt to hear she'd been pretending to be someone she wasn't, I can't let that stop me from taking a leap of faith and trusting her again.

Dee's right: if I carry on pushing everyone away, I'll never be happy.

Feeling an urgent need to sort this whole mess out as quickly as possible, I pull my mobile out of my pocket, look up Bea's number and tap out a text, asking her to meet me here.

* * *

She doesn't reply right away and I pace through the grounds, past the lake, feeling a swell of love for the place again now that my strongest memory there is of playing in the water with Bea – and of the way she kissed me, even though she knew she shouldn't. She did it anyway. Because she couldn't not. Just like I can't not be with her.

I make it over to the apple orchard before my phone buzzes and I slide it out of my pocket, my heart in my mouth as I open the reply and read it.

She's coming. Right now.

Relief floods through me and I flop onto the ground by one of the largest trees and put my head into my hands, listening to the blood rushing in my ears as my heart pumps it hard through my veins.

Thank God.

After finally electing to stop being such a dick and contact her, I'd immediately become terrified she'd decide she didn't want anything to do with me after all and would refuse to come over. So her acceptance is extremely welcome.

Not that I know for sure that this thing between us is salvageable. She might still turn up just to tell me to sod off.

I guess I wouldn't blame her, after the way I acted when we'd slept together.

The mere memory of it has me immediately hard and I have a visceral flash of the way she smelled, the softness of her skin under my touch and the small moans of pleasure she let out as I slid inside her.

Jeez.

I've been trying so hard not to think about that. How I felt before, during and after it. Just how much I wanted it to happen again. But I've been battling with my ego ever since and punishing myself – and her – for things that don't matter any more.

She matters though. *We* matter.

We're good together. More than good.

I need to pull myself together before she gets here though or I'm not going to be able to speak to her without stumbling over my words in my rush to be able to touch her again.

Somehow, even in the short time I've known her, she's been able to turn my world upside down. Or maybe right it. Performing with her gave me back the feeling of joy I used to experience when playing my guitar and for me, that's massive. But – just for the moment at least – I only want to perform for her. Share the intimacy of musically connecting – with her.

I get up and pace around the orchard, my nerves humming.

I don't know exactly what I'm going to say to her once she gets here, but I'm sure as soon as I see her, it'll become clear. I know I want her back in my life. And hopefully, I'll be able to persuade her to come back to Gladbrooke in some capacity, even if she's not working here any more.

After what seems like an endless twenty more minutes, my phone finally buzzes with a text and I look at it and see she's arrived and is asking where to find me. I drop her a pin and sit back down to wait for her to emerge through the trees.

It doesn't take her long to make it over to where I am and my heart soars when I first hear the crunch of her feet on the hard earth, then see her walking through the orchard towards me.

Getting to my feet, I brush bits of soil off my jeans and try to adopt a relaxed-looking stance as she draws nearer.

As she gets closer, I can see her expression is one of strained worry and I feel a surge of guilt for causing her that pain. I'd thought that meeting in the trees would be romantic, but from the stiff way she's moving, she's clearly wondering what the hell I've got planned here.

So I stride towards her, making sure I put as much warmth into my smile as I can.

This seems to have the right effect, because the frown drops from her face and she gives me a heartbreakingly tentative smile in return.

Seeing this just about breaks me and without another thought, the moment I reach her, I lift my hands to her face and draw her towards me, kissing her hard.

There's no hesitation on her part either; she kisses me back with just as much passion and purpose and we sink against each other's bodies, our arms wrapped tightly around each other, as if we're afraid to let go in case we lose each other again.

It's so absolutely right, her being here with me, kissing beneath the apple trees.

'I'm sorry I pushed you away,' I mutter against her lips, once we finally break apart for breath. 'I was afraid I was being made a fool of again, even though I knew, deep down, you'd never do that to me. My fear of rejection got the better of me.'

She pulls back a little to smile at me. 'I totally understand. And I don't blame you for the way you reacted. I probably would have done just the same if I'd been in your shoes.' I see her swallow. 'But you do believe that I never meant to lie to you and hurt you, don't you? I really thought I was doing a good thing for everyone when I first came here. But I messed up by not being able to leave. I pushed it too far and ended up having to lie to cover my bad choices and I'm truly sorry for that.' My skin tingles as she cups my face. 'I fell in love with you.'

I can tell from the expression in her eyes that she really means that.

'I love you too,' I say, completely certain that I do. How could

I not? She's absolutely perfect for me and I can't imagine never seeing or being with her again. My life would be very much more the poorer for not having her in it.

The look she gives me now is full of relief and pure joy. 'Thank goodness,' she murmurs, her voice sounding a little hoarse, as if the emotion of the situation has got the better of her and she's holding back happy tears.

'Let's sit down,' I suggest, gesturing to a patch of soft-looking grass under one of the trees.

She nods in agreement and we sit down, so close our bodies are pressed together from the tops of our arms to our thighs. Sliding a hand along her back, then cupping her shoulder, I pull her in even closer to my body and kiss the top of her head, breathing in the wonderful, familiar, sweet scent of her.

'You know, because of my dad's fame, I've always felt like my relationships were conditional. That my partner was only with me because of it. Tessa was the perfect example of that. She was clearly a music groupie, I knew that from the moment I met her, but I fell for her hard anyway. I know, I've been screwed up about what happened with her and it made me paranoid, but when I found out about you and Dee, I was afraid the two of you were playing some sort of game with me. When Dee failed at getting my attention, you stepped in and took over. I actually thought you might be the "good cop" to Dee's "bad cop" to mess with my head.'

She shoots me a wry smile. 'Honestly, it was almost impossible to act as if I didn't find you incredibly attractive whenever I was around you. It was actually torture, especially when you started paying me more attention and I knew I couldn't return it. I wanted to so much.'

'Same. It nearly killed me to stay professional around you.'

We look at each other now and our gazes lock. There's such

heat in her eyes, such need. I feel it too, thrumming in the air between us.

I've never experienced this kind of intensity with anyone else and it's the best feeling in the world.

Glancing down at her mouth, I see it curving into a smile. Without another thought, I lean in and press my lips against hers, feeling them open under mine and I slip my tongue into the heat of her mouth and run my fingers into her hair.

This is exactly what my body's been craving since the last time we touched and it's the sweetest feeling to be able to have it again.

I'm never letting her go.

'What made you change your mind about seeing me again?' she asks when we come up for air.

'Your sister coming over to read me the riot act,' I say, smoothing down the front of her now rather wild-looking hair, 'and for once in my life, I listened, then gave myself a talking to about how I'd been behaving – like a bloody stroppy child. It helped that it was Dee that said it to me though. Seeing her made me miss you even more.'

She lets out a surprised snort. 'I never thought it'd be my sister fixing my relationship for me. It's always been the other way round with us. But something's clearly happened to her recently to make her grow up a bit.'

'Really?'

'Yeah. I don't know what, but I intend to get it out of her the moment I see her again.'

'Intriguing.'

She grins at me, her eyes alive with happiness. It's a beautiful sight.

'Thank you for giving me another chance.'

The sincerity in her voice sends an arrow of guilt through my chest.

'Yeah, well. I figured I was being an idiot to let what happened to me in the past inform what happens to me in the future. Especially if it meant losing you. I'd much rather lose face than lose you.' I huff out an embarrassed laugh. 'Listen to me, I sound like an inspirational bloody quote again.'

'I know exactly what you're saying,' she says, hugging me tightly.

'Good. Because I guess life is messy. Love is messy. Nothing and no-one is perfect. I get that and I'm prepared to figure it out with you because I love you. You were right, we are meant to be together; I genuinely feel that.'

'So you forgive me?'

'Yes. Because I know the lies came from a good place. I'm in awe and, honestly, jealous of your love and devotion to your sister. I don't feel like anyone's ever given me those things the way you have to Dee. And I want that for myself. From you. I want in, Bea.'

'Well then, you're in, because that's exactly what I want too. I think we can give each other what we need.'

'But if we're going to make this work, we both have to promise not to lie to each other again.'

'I promise.'

'I promise too.'

'Good. Well, that's sorted then. Let's do everything we can to make this work.'

'Agreed.'

'I'm excited.'

'Me too.'

'I can't wait to put all our plans into action.'

'Speaking of action...' I waggle my eyebrows at her. 'I wouldn't mind getting some more of that right now.'

'What? Here under the tree?' she asks, her eyebrows raised in mock outrage.

'Sure, why not? I intend to have sex with you all over this estate and we may as well start right here.'

Her laugh rings out into the cool, fresh air around us. It's the most beautiful thing I've heard since I last heard her singing.

'All over the estate? That's a lot of ground to cover.'

'Then we'd better get started,' I say, pulling her towards me again and kissing her hard, feeling her body respond.

And I know for certain that this time, I'm with exactly the right person at the right time – that we both want the same things – and it's only going to get better from here.

EPILOGUE
THREE YEARS LATER

Beatrice

I wake up to the low hum of electric vans trundling down the driveway to the hotel and pulling into the empty car park, ready to disgorge their loads.

Rubbing the sleep out of my eyes, I yawn and stretch, then reach out to the space next to me in the bed. It's empty. Jonah must already be up and out, ready to greet the festival crew as they begin their set-up of the next Terra Firmer festival to be hosted here at Gladbrooke House.

He's obviously let me sleep in a bit this morning but has left me a still-hot cup of coffee on the bedside table.

I love him so much.

He's such a thoughtful, generous man.

I can barely believe how I got so lucky some days.

Our relationship has gone from strength to strength since that day in the apple orchard – not that there hasn't been the odd occasion when we've wanted to throttle each other, like all couples. Running the hotel has been stressful at times, especially in the early days when we were struggling to turn a profit.

But we found a way to work through it and I'm so glad we stuck with it.

Sitting up, I take a long sip from the mug, feeling the fragrant liquid warm my throat and stomach.

Glorious.

I swing my legs out of bed and walk over to the window of our cottage, peering out between a gap in the curtains.

The sun is out in full force, making the dew-soaked grass shimmer. I can't help but smile as I gaze out across the lawns to the clay tennis courts that have been recently upgraded. I can see Jonah shaking hands after a game with Ben, one of the hotel staff he gets on with particularly well.

I watch as he makes his way back over to the entrance to the hotel, where Jay is getting out of one of the trucks, a hand held aloft in greeting.

Jonah looks so happy – absolutely in his element, in fact – his gorgeous face relaxed and his eyes shining with pleasure at the sight of our friend.

I, too, still get excited when I see Jay and his entourage arriving with all the glamping tents, marquees and catering supplies. It's always a joy to have them here.

In the last three years, we've hosted seven different events for him here and each time they've got bigger – helped by some brilliant reviews, both from influencers and from some of the traditional news outlets. They're not on the scale of Glastonbury – not that we could even think about hosting something that large – but they're now big enough to be highly profitable, which means we're able to charge a very pleasing fee.

The knock-on publicity from Terra Firmer has also meant that we're now fully booked for the rest of the year, even in low season, with guests wanting to stay at the hotel where it's held. It's actually turning into a bit of a celebrity get-away, with some pretty influential people booking the whole place out for weeks at a time.

My idea to turn the lake into a place for picnics, wild swimming and boating has had a really positive effect too, with people citing it as one of the main reasons they loved staying here. It gives the place an especially retro-British feel, apparently.

In fact, last year, we had a film crew use the house and grounds as a location for a period drama, which came out a month ago. It was a big box-office hit, so it's also driven up the number of enquiries from people who want to visit the 'movie set'.

After months of intensive research and networking, Jonah managed to get the funding we needed to start up the cider press and it's gone from strength to strength – both the business and the cider. But because he went tee-total three years ago – with the support of a local AA group – and hasn't had a drink since, he leaves the tasting of it to his colleagues.

He's loved getting his teeth into a new project and has been happy leaving the running of the hotel and rest of the grounds to me.

Once we started turning a profit, I was able to start updating the remaining rooms so we're now able to accommodate even more guests.

I've also been looking into opening a separate restaurant here for people who aren't staying at the hotel, which will be housed in a purpose-built annex. We're intending to use produce grown on our land, along with goods from local suppliers and perhaps even have a small farm shop too.

But that's all to come.

A shiver of pleasure runs through me at the thought of what the future holds.

Moving away from the window, I go and take a quick shower in our en suite, then pull on some of the festival clothes Jonah and I have begun building a wardrobe of, so we can blend in with the festivities and feel more of a part of what's happening.

We're able to pay staff members to keep on top of whatever Jay and his team might need while the festival's running now, which means Jonah and I are free to get involved in the workshops and performances if we want to.

Which we usually do.

In fact, Jonah's played a set during the cabaret at every festival so far and has roped me in to sing with him for most of them too, which I've loved.

There's something so special about performing with him. So connecting.

I adore listening to him playing his guitar in our home too, which he does nearly every day. He's even started doing small, local gigs in some of the pubs nearby, which are always sold out.

He's adamant he doesn't want to be a career musician any more though, so this way, he can really enjoy playing without the pressure to compete with, or be compared to, his rock-star father.

I actually got to meet his dad a year ago. He was very charming, very friendly, but not always emotionally present for Jonah, often acting as if he was just another person in his entourage, which helped make a lot of Jonah's behaviours and choices make sense to me.

Superstardom seems to be an addiction of Jim Jacobson's, even more so than alcohol, and brings with it extreme highs and lows that keep him on a different wavelength to everyone else.

It was a fascinating insight into something I don't ever want to be a part of.

Thankfully, neither does Jonah.

We're both extremely happy with our life here at Gladbrooke House.

The place truly feels like home to me now, which it has been since I moved in with Jonah two and a half years ago.

I've never felt so content. At peace. As if I'm in exactly the right place with exactly the right person.

I count myself *very* lucky.

I've not said as much to Jonah, but I suspect Tessa is kicking herself now for indulging in such a cruel and public break-up with him because she's now not able to visit the place alongside her celebrity and influencer friends.

Not that Jonah's banned her or anything.

But I can't imagine she'd be welcomed with open arms by anyone here.

He's actually much more chilled about the messy break-up with Tessa now. In fact, he's even able to laugh about it with people if they ever dare mention the Reverse Darcy thing.

He decided to own it and it's taken the sting out of it for him.

I'm so proud of him.

And myself, if I'm honest.

My dad took a bit of time to come around to my change in career direction and our relationship was a bit fractious for a while. He eventually agreed to meet Jonah and come over to Gladbrooke to look around though and of course, once he saw what a great job we were making of it, and more importantly, how much happier I am now, he reluctantly admitted I'd made a good choice.

He really likes Jonah too. He can see how good he is for me.

And he really is.

Just as I'm thinking this, Jonah strolls in through the front door and comes straight over to me, pulling me into his arms and kissing me hard.

'Morning, beautiful. I see you're already ready to party,' he says, smiling into my eyes.

I'll never get bored with seeing that smile.

An excited shiver of anticipation runs through me. 'I certainly am. Are you getting ready too now?'

He shakes his head. 'I need to make a few calls, then I need to speak to Tony about some repairs to the cider press, but I'll catch up with you after that and we can practice the set for tonight.'

'Great.'

I smile and lean in for another kiss, luxuriating in the firm press of his mouth against mine. Breathing in his delicious, unique scent, I feel my body rush with desire and almost suggest we head back to bed before he leaves again.

But we have too much to do this morning. It'll have to wait.

Reluctantly, I draw away from him and extract myself from his arms.

'Is Dee coming tonight?' he asks, running a hand through his now slightly dishevelled hair.

'Yup. That's the plan.'

He nods, then drops a soft kiss onto the top of my head.

'It'll be great to see her. It's been ages.'

He's right. It has.

My sister and I have taken very different paths and we don't get to see each other much these days. It's always a joy to be around her whenever we do get together though, especially now she's taking full responsibility for her life. She and my dad still have a difficult relationship, to say the least, but both of them try hard to get on when we're all together, which I appreciate.

'She's looking forward to seeing you too and she promises to be on her best behaviour and not make any more bad jokes about you being an apple farmer,' I say with an ironic tilt of my eyebrow.

'I don't believe that for a second,' Jonah says with a grin, before walking back out of the door and heading towards his office to make those calls.

I watch him out of the window as he strides away from me, my body still craving his touch. He cuts a striking figure as he moves through the growing number of festival crew members, who all greet him warmly as he passes.

No matter how much time we spend together, I never get tired of being around him. He's such an intrinsic part of my life now I can't imagine doing it without him. I definitely have a sense of my life being split into two halves. Before Jonah and With Jonah.

My heart swells with love in my chest and I experience a rush of pure joy.

I almost want to run after him and tell him how much love I'm feeling for him right now.

Later. I'll get him all to myself later, once the festival's heading to bed and my sister has left for the night.

I smile as my thoughts turn to all that's happened to Dee in the last few years.

She's in a much better place and situation all round now, which I'm delighted about. Surprisingly, she's really turned her life around with the help of the one person I thought I'd never see her getting together with.

If you'd asked me a few years ago where I envisioned Dee ending up, I never would have guessed the direction or partner she's chosen.

I'm very glad she did though.

It was quite a challenge at the beginning, apparently, but one she's really stepped up to.

But that's a whole other story.

ACKNOWLEDGEMENTS

Writing, for me, has always been a pleasure, but also a cathartic release – especially when life has thrown me curve-balls – so I'm incredibly lucky to have such a supportive, loving family, who have always been so encouraging about my chosen career. A huge thank you must go to them for keeping me sane.

Thanks also, as ever, to my wonderful editor, Megan. Such a pleasure to work with you and the rest of the Boldwood team.

And of course, to you, the reader. I very much appreciate you choosing to read my stories. I hope they bring you joy.

ABOUT THE AUTHOR

Christy McKellen is the author of provocative and sexy romance novels that have sold over half a million copies worldwide.

Sign up to Christy McKellen's mailing list for news, competitions and updates on future books.

Visit Christy's website: www.christymckellen.com

Follow Christy on social media here:

f facebook.com/christymckellenauthor
X x.com/ChristyMcKellen
📷 instagram.com/christymckellen
BB bookbub.com/authors/christy-mckellen

ALSO BY CHRISTY MCKELLEN

Three's a Crowd

Marry Me...Maybe?

About Last Night

Best Mistake Ever

LOVE NOTES

LOVE IN EVERY CHAPTER

WHERE ALL YOUR ROMANCE
DREAMS COME TRUE!

THE HOME OF BESTSELLING
ROMANCE AND WOMEN'S
FICTION

WARNING:
MAY CONTAIN SPICE

Boldwood

Boldwood Books is an award-winning fiction publishing company seeking out the best stories from around the world.

Find out more at www.boldwoodbooks.com

Join our reader community for brilliant books, competitions and offers!

Follow us
@BoldwoodBooks
@TheBoldBookClub

Sign up to our weekly deals newsletter

https://bit.ly/BoldwoodBNewsletter